ONE

Meat is not dead flesh; it retains all the sufferings and assumes all the colors of living flesh. It manifests such convulsive pain and vulnerability, but also such delightful invention, color, and acrobatics.

—Gilles Deleuze,
Francis Bacon: The Logic of Sensation

ONE

Written by
Blake Butler & Vanessa Place

Assembled by
Christopher Higgs

Roof Books
New York

ISBN: 978-1-931824-47-7
Library of Congress Catalog Card Number: 2012948275

State of the Arts NYSCA This book was made possible, in part, with public funds from the New York State Council on the Arts, a state agency.

Roof Books are distributed by
Small Press Distribution
1341 Seventh Street
Berkeley, CA. 94710-1403
Phone orders: 800-869-7553
www.spdbooks.org

Roof Books are published by
Segue Foundation
300 Bowery
New York, NY 10012
seguefoundation.com

Table of Contents

Foreword

What you are about to read is the product of a collaborative experiment: what if one writer (Vanessa Place) wrote a narrative composed entirely from the interior landscape of a character while another writer (Blake Butler) wrote a narrative composed entirely from the exterior landscape of a character, neither writer communicating with the other until both writers gave their finished product to another writer (Christopher Higgs, Me) who would then assemble the two narratives together to form one unified piece?

The project originated in the fall of 2009, while I was studying Alfred Jarry's 'Pataphysics, reading Kenneth Goldsmith's *Fidget*, and watching a gluttonous amount of Jean-Luc Godard films. My work at the time revolved around an obsession with remixing preexisting material, specifically turning stage plays into prose poems. The idea for this book arose from those conditions.

One night in October, I emailed Blake to explain the basic premise and ask if he might be interested in participating. He agreed to join the project and enthusiastically encouraged me to pursue it. Soon thereafter I contacted Vanessa to ask if she might be interested. Unlike Blake, with whom I had a prior relationship, contacting Vanessa was a shot in the dark. I sent her a long email, introducing myself and the concept for the project, which concluded with, "What do you think? I know this probably sounds absolutely insane, especially because you & I don't know each other, but I'm hoping you might look past those minor glitches." Shortly thereafter Vanessa replied, "Dear Chris, I adore minor glitches, and the project sounds like potential fun. In spite of that, I'm in."

With both writers on board, I turned my attention toward finalizing the details of the project, so Blake and Vanessa could begin to compose. As I explained to them, I envisioned the basic premise of the experiment in terms of 4.1 constraints, with an additional, individual constraint for each of them. The initial underlying questions I had been interested in exploring involved the relationship between interior and exterior, subject and object, as well as the connection and separation of those two aspects of existence. My hope at the time was that when I merged their two separate texts to create the unified document something magical might be achieved that could only have been produced by this particular process. Here are the 4.1 Basic Constraints, given to both Blake and Vanessa:

1) First Person
2) Present tense
3) Compose ~40-60 pages
Avoid discussing the details with one another
4.1) Because I want to avoid prefabricated cohesion, while at the same time I feel the need to offer a framework within which to play, I'll suggest that you think in terms of three movements: Discovery –Secrecy – Escape. These need not be sequential, in other words feel free to think in terms of Escape – Discovery – Secrecy, or whatever arrangement of those you want. My hope is that by suggesting these three specific movements it will give you helpful boundary demarcations, and also it will allow me to locate common vector points at which I might establish pivots for the final construction.

In terms of individual constraints, I asked Blake to focus on exteriority, on depicting movements of the body in space, setting, location, objects, interactions, and so on, while refraining from anything related to interiority: thoughts, memories, emotions, motivations, and so on. I asked Vanessa to focus on interiority, on those things I had restricted Blake from using, and asked her to refrain from anything related to exteriority.

Beyond those constraints, I gave them free rein to produce whatever they desired. I had no idea what they would produce, and even less of an idea as to how well their two radically dissimilar texts might work in concert with one another. What I did know was that I greatly admired both writers and felt confident that their shared passion for language would hybridize nicely.

After a few months, I received their individual documents. Immediately I began to study them, chart their trajectories, identify their affinities, and note their particular patterns of repetition, in order to get a sense of how and in what ways their separate narratives might imbricate. I found particularly interesting the ways in which they chose to negotiate their constraints. What it demonstrated to me was the apparent impossibility of the project, the limits of attempting to separate internalities and externalities, which gave me all the more reason to pursue it. Could I, as the creator of the combined text, bring these individual pieces together to form a functioning whole? And if so, what would this new text look like?

The assembling process began weeks later, after I felt I had a strong familiarity with both pieces, and a sense of where I would begin and where I would end. If I remember correctly, the opening of the book came from the latter part of Vanessa's narrative and the ending of the book came from the latter part of Blake's narrative. Between those two poles, the chronology of the final product had little to do with the chronology presented to me by the individual primary texts. It also became apparent as I began to assemble the text that my initial suggestion about using the three movements Escape – Discovery – Secrecy might actually manifest itself more messily than I anticipated: secrecy bleeding into escape and discovery bleeding into secrecy. So instead of relying on those demarcations, I chose to utilize a more fluid partitioning device: the "Utterance," which originally came, I believe, from Blake's text, but then underwent the same morphing and mashing together with Vanessa's text as the rest.

As I gave them constraints, I also gave myself a constraint. I was not allowed to type anything with my own keyboard. I was only allowed to copy and paste. Every word, therefore, comes from either Blake or Vanessa. The arrangement of their words, however, comes from me.

So we three are its creator, from the house within the dream house, the helmet shackling us to memories of our father, we remember the evolution of law in order to help create stability as we continually struggle with our doppelganger who too must necessarily be some embodiment or figment of multiplicity trapped between the material and immaterial.

What follows, then, the product of our experiment, could be described as a grotesque symphony of chimerical language, a fever dream of somatic isolation that depicts the gore of loneliness arising from persistent waking nightmares and an obsession with the history of jurisprudence. As a textual body, you may consider our text akin to Frankenstein's creation. Recall, if you will, the way Shelley describes the creature as an amalgam of materials "from the dissecting room and the slaughter-house," and perhaps conceive of Blake as the slaughter-house and Vanessa as the dissecting table, or vice versa. Of course, that makes me the Doctor, the unpardonable villain.

Christopher Higgs
Tallahassee, June 2012

I Utterance One

A dream house in a dream city, dreaming of the future and reversible destiny

OR:

Trial by Ordeal; Trial by Battle

[•]

One has a plan. One did not have a plan previously, when the dimensions of one's situation were not known to one. This is always the case. Say something to remember. Say something by which one would remember. Say never again, again. Plans are made retrospectively, if they have any hope of working at all.

I have to know how to get back here when I am done with wherever else there is.

One has considered a schematic representation of one's situation, which is no more euphemism than the predicate possessive pronoun, and in this way reminds one of a dream one once had about a man with one leg who insisted on riding a bicycle.

Memorize: I say I say I say I said, one method of flight involves the creation of the simulacrum, often out of bits of whatnot, soap, lather, foam, hair, air, oysters and thatch. Soot is also good, if one can find a hearth. If no hearth, wait till the next Lent and stand in line five or six times. You can also simply weep till ashen.

One day, perhaps the story of the family will be told, and how they came to be in the various institutions. There were numerous complaints that various authorities had exceeded their power. One is a proud people, though pointless.

Here's a joke. Stop if one's heard it before. Equity grew in its desire to deal with the *de facto* failings of the common law courts, and did not concern itself with doctrinal differences. Acts of jurisprudence, again. Of justice. Again. As one was saying, one day there was a one-legged man on a bicycle riding by, one swore it was one's father, it looked just like him, from this perspective, of course, that is to say. Horizontal. Lateral. When in relation, as he used to say—what was it? Something about a bicycle.

But stop one if one has heard this one. A one-legged man is riding a bicycle when he comes across—one's father, horizontal. It was bound to happen, an accident like that. There's nothing like alterity. Nothing at all. Fate, in other words. Does the other believe? Naturally. What's not to? Nothing. Nothing doing. If one had a nickel for every bit of nothing one cradled and put to bed, there'd be a sea of change, that's all. Don't mistake this, though, for one does love a bit of nothing. Warm nothing, nothing with syrup. Say nothing. Say no more. Nothing for nothing, that's what one's father used to say. How the other could laugh as he rode by on his bicycle. One should like a sequence of numbers played at this moment, a-harmonically, as if this were possible. There's harmonics in it, all the others say so. For example, returning back, as if there were another way or direction to it, referring back one means to say, referring back to one's earlier statement on equation. Take a simple proposition, one sure to warm the cockles of any well-tended member. Such as, dogs are like people. No argument there. From petting to pounding, and happily brown-eyed in between. Dogs are like people, ergo people are like dogs. There. Mathematically proven. Collar 'em, leash 'em, license 'em, implant chips for their safe relocation. Call them Jake, Princess, and one's own true bitch, it's all well-organized. This is the great fact of epistemology, by which is meant mathematics. Truth is math, math is truth, not understanding one, except for in the grossest, simplest formulations, makes one a better one. Truer, as if the eyes were bluer. Impossible. There is none more azure eye than I. I've a critique du rhythme, counted out in the metronome of an augenblich, nicht, nicht-ich, nicht, nicht-ich.

Lovely. It must be getting on a quarter of there. Or somewhere. Surely we can submeasure in minutes, if we can grasp the hours. Often, a suitor who was dissatisfied with the result in a common law court would refile the case in Equity or Chancery. This seems to be the point, at least from where one squats, to seize the mechanism by which the other parcels out one's particulars. As previously mentioned. One mentions the particulars because they have that grainy quality so common to the commonplace. Like old photos. Non-existent, in other words. Like in other words. Like old photos. One has to admit of something. Speaking only for oneself, one can allow as one has been many places, and hopes for more. Say thirty-one. Then again, there's also the call of no place in particular, or rather in particular, no place. As one was saying, this is a mathematical proposition, a measure of means, meaning: meaning. When one was younger one had various items that one would associate with mathematics, imaginary items to be sure, but real nonetheless—four pieces of chocolate plus three pieces of candy equals what, if one has six jacks and two hands, and one gives a red ball to another, what does one have on hand, and so on. The point is there was methodology, by which is meant taxonomy, and this is where liberation begins. Systems. Plans. No secrets. No troves for treasuring. Things to be spoken *of*. These latter courts saw their role as being 'equalizers': socially, legally, economically. In this position, and encouraged by Roman law traditions, they were always creative in producing new writs which could not be found in the common law courts. Good as done. Like lunch on a Monday evening or a fresh set of slippers, the plastic loop looping them together still in situ. There's a French word for it, meaning *avole*. As one recalls, it was Tuesday one had lunch last. No supper. Sardines in tomato sauce, with a salad of wild rice and fava beans. One wishes. Feta or somesuch was introduced to collegial effect. The sardines went off while one was eating, which lead to this, the plan. Subtraction. The take-away. It was in this spirit that Justice Berrewyk in 1302, ordered an infant to be brought before the court with a writ subpoena: 'under pain of (forefeit) of 100 pounds'. The less as lessor, the entailment being another form of more. So that if there is growth, there will necessarily be elimination. Take cancer, for example. Take the rising tide of public sentiment and the corresponding lack of real feeling. Take two, if you like. There's a mesh tote bag available at the front desk, if there was a front desk. Due to the recent decrease in funding, one has had to make due with simply leaving a small side window open during business hours, which one no longer has. The other saves a tremendous amount of money by spending more—see how the logic is impeccable. But there is evidence that 'threat of penalty' had been attached to writs used by the government to induce behavior as early as 1232. It's all a matter of product placement, and the strategic use of feta cheese.

[•]

And so my day begins again, again. Where I think into this evening, I hear me in the mash around my head. I eat corn, bacon, and candy. The helmets here are heavy and cause the stoop. My spine hurts, like a living diamond ladder, with no handles and no rungs.

It could be less so. It can always be less so. No more so than less so. Meaning: no more but less. Leaving all the more. Less, that is. Again.

Suppose this is the way of any number of things. Say thirty-seven. Say writs of many kinds formed the essential parts of litigation. Say thirty-nine. Say the primary function of a writ in the 13th and 14th centuries was to convey the king's commands to his officers and servants. Don't say the other. It was irrelevant what the nature of those commands might be. Mustn't say the other. Never again—again.

Here, still, in this unending evening, I lift my head hard enough to see outside the night. I can hold my glance position only for several seconds, noticing three things:

(a) Someone scratching sky off.
(b) Another body.
(c) Floor.

What a floor is here is a pile of shit that I have yet to stick my head in, while the sky is still a sock. As for the other body, when I can make the urge again to see again, it's gone. Though sometimes there is some rummage in my sternum, and sometimes rope around my throat.

Remember this: the Register of Writs shows a large variety of writs to be administrative in nature, as opposed to judicial. These former writs acquired the name prerogative writs in the 17th and 18th centuries. This is certain, being history. Still, it's a sort of shadow, really, though not so cumbersome. Lighter and yet much quieter than one expected. An aerial view. Suspected, one should say. One may assert. Prerogative writs that have survived into modern law are the *writ of mandamus* and *writ of certiorari.* One might aver. Still, more or less quiet, at any rate. More or less light, that is to say.

These three things that I can see and I don't want to, for how the helmet makes me poor, makes me chew the hell out of the inside of my lip, which fills my mouth again with pus, which swims around my teeth and tongue where the words come from, really, shiftskin, and I am spitting up the blood. On the floor of shit this house has the blood pools in a picture of this house. These walls gleaming in their seizures make no sound in me at all.

I smell the sun around my helmet in the evening while the sun's not even here. A second helmet for my helmet, another day drummed to beginning.

There is no helmet here at all ever but I prefer to say there is, to have a window for this evening through which I am looking out onto the smudgefold to see when someone is coming over the pig bodies and the bleat. The bridges of this city of so many glowing skylines, each one strung from somewhere else.

In the dumb hiding of this house's hours I wrap my hands one round the other to make pray, which takes the whole day again and even then some, and after that, I need to sleep.

Before drifting off, one smelt the overwhelming smelt of remembered apples—doesn't it sound like something? Something sans regard. Something wounded. Wounding. Same difference, if the nails are kept well.

Say the medieval writ of prohibition played an important part in the conflict between the church and state in England. At any rate, say daily, say weekly, say hourly. Don't say the other. What kind of provocation, that's the question. The writ was also used in the courts of admiralty and local courts. It has survived in relative obscurity in United States law. This is after writing, though what manner of having written. Through, that is to say.

In the hall I front assume the Z position, my knees denting my headmeat.

These are days here. This is the knocking. I hear someone in the house say, without sound, "Yesterday I will do the same thing I did I did again again."

My voice walks up behind me, taps me on the head.

Today I believe I am very funny and I tell whoever is behind me in the hall. The writ subpoena began to be attached to a wide variety of writs in the 1300s. These were an invention of the Court of Equity, which were a part of Chancery. In the light along the bending husk of walls and ceilings, the floor reflects the other parts of place around it so I can walk around and yet as all days become restraining and all hours are the clog, I give up before I can begin. Thus, 'subpoena' was a product of the Ecclesiastical Courts in England. I'm down. This is the last time I will tell you when I'm curling. Otherwise, assume the practice of hiding information from certain individuals or groups, perhaps while sharing it with other individuals, as if wanted, as if needed, as if desire. Whatever, that is.

Heretical. Blaspheme. Spam. The commonest writ from this era was the *Praecipe quod reddat* (You are commanded to return [some misappropriated good or land]). That which is kept hidden is known as this, as to these were often added the phrase: *sub poena*. You wish. Cum silentio. Then there'd be proof of something. Whenever there's nothing, there's sure to be proof of something. Whatever, that is, I say I say I say I said.

A portrait on the far wall where I am headed mostly is right there. As I approach with my helmet, I can make out a little of the shape of what's been made: a picture of a person with two heads to his or her name, a person looking both ways at once, before another panel of other eyes. Mirrors hung up around the eyes to seem many all at once.

The eyes set in the wall will not blink unless I am not looking.

This is the night.

When I wake and find my gut uncut I stand up inside this unending day and thrust again.

In the kitchen, with the knife set and the oven, I sit and make a list of my whole life. I write with two pencils at the same time, so when one tip breaks I will not be disrupted. I have a hold. My both hands go on crawling.

Often controversial, depending on the content, the group or people, the motivation *for* the development of the writ subpoena is closely associated with the invention of due process, which slowly replaced trial by ordeal. They say 'matter of fact' casually, as if leaning against a wall outside something else. It's the measure of things. Ongoing. Imperative. Edifice rex. Lex talon. It's all the same.

My life is wine, or it is money. My hands will not stay still—and yet each word I write comes out of me as backwards or crossed through or upside down. No matter how hard I help to hold my pencil straight up and on point. Nowhere in this, as I said: knocking.

And so my day begins again, again.

This day's day comes on as if meant to be remembered gooing in a loop: I ask. I bark. I crawl. I draw. I drink. I eat. I fuck. I grow wide. I have anger. I... I... I insist. I itch. I justify. I krush. I kill. I love the way I smell. I love the crust upon the morning. I mime. I mind. I never laugh. I open tiny doors. I owe. I punch my chest. I quit. I quit. I quote, "The dome itself was not actually complete." I run straight into a door. I rush anything worth not rushing. I rut until my holes are sore. I say nothing I ever meant to say. I tongue the sores inside my mind. I trust everybody. I um. I undo. I want and want. I wish I knew why. I wish I knew why I wish I knew why. I wish I wasn't. I xxx. I yearn. I zzz. So what the fuck.

In the slur of any of me, I stand and walk across the gleaming floor, its face, again, repeating, in the blips where I can blink, and thereby see where I am headed, a pencil still crammed in each hand.

Say thirteen. The institution of the jury trial necessitated the hearing of evidence. There's a hope. One. This, in turn led to the need for a reliable method of compelling witnesses to appear and give testimony. Two. Often decried as excessive or in promotion of poor operation; note: excessive revelation of hope has the taste of undercooked chicken. Thus, the writ subpoena became the standard method of compelling witnesses.

My cells will not sit still. Even in the mode of going horizontal: to be filled up or let down.

Inside the helmet, again, instead of writing, I add lines to the center of the face. Today I make more shading on the upper lip, where hair has begun to grow. I do not remember making hair. I try to shave it with the pencil's upper edge, combing down in long strokes with my both arms at the same time, as if the face and I are fighting.

One shouldn't wonder. Following the Fourth Lateran Council in 1215 and based on a Latin interpretation of natural moral law, all forms of trial by ordeal or trial by battle were outlawed in Church courts. The elegance of order is too easy, though this does not diminish either its attraction or its merit.

Soon I am bleeding down both arms. Of greater significance to English law was the fact that the clergy were banned from blessing trial by ordeal in the civil and common law courts. This had the effect of bringing the practice of trial by ordeal to an abrupt halt in England. Never again. Again. Mustn't again, no more. Trial by battle, which later evolved into a method of settling scores by dueling, was less affected. Can conflict with virtues of privacy and confidentiality spread to soak? The blood pours on the carpet, spreads to soak it. Through the helmet I watch it make a map—a little trail leading from me to the front door to whatever shit aligns the lane. My front stoop made of blue bones. My grassyard high as me. Good, the blood a little conduit etching a way out of my house.

[•]

Note to self: never again, again. Note to another: one more time.

Trial by ordeal had always been viewed with skepticism and condescension by Latin lawyers and intelligentsia. My blood does bubbles that have sounds about them, like someone talking who is deaf, and cannot hear. Often, there is a landscape. If it is populated, it becomes something else. The crack of my lips makes flakes upon the living room that settles on the blood as ships, and therein flows down from me in the current, a flow out from one ocean to the next.

On a deeper level, humans attempt to conceal aspects of their own self which they are not capable of incorporating psychologically into their conscious being.

Trial by battle, for the sake of honor had a long and proud tradition in Rome, and remained prominent in Roman lands. One must eat something. This is the secret of success in business. Still, it had been banned by the Church courts on the Continent. Those who wanted to duel simply ignored the ban. True, as far as it goes. It was generally believed that God's will was revealed in the outcome of the battle or ordeal. The fact that the judge would view the result of the ordeal and declare 'God's decision' had little bearing on the validity of the procedure.

God, if you can hear it: someone is beating the shit out of the roof.

The rings on both my middle fingers glisten.

Following the Fourth Lateran Council, the civil and common law courts quickly moved to ban these practices, as well. One never tells. Never can tell, that is to say. Many are maintained by using a mutually agreed-upon construct (an official family story) when speaking with outside members. It would be nice to talk in peace and quiet. Nonetheless, implementation proved to be more difficult. What to replace trial by ordeal and trial by combat *with*? I watch my blood erupt and gutter, harden, form a fissure, a dripping dais, from which I hear a bunch of trumpets, and then the dais sinks back into the fat. The globules on my blood's flow make pretty patchwork. I start to step from one to one to one to one and further onward, further on right out of my whole house. The information may even be something as trivial as a recipe. Something as major as a general. Something inappropriate as that. Medium, as existence. Das Ding-Ding. Say plus one. The novel choice was trial by jury. Where from? Erratum. Remember: keeping one's strategy is important in many aspects of game theory. Shouldn't wonder.

At the front door I stop a little, think of locking, think of going back to bed. I don't. Outside the day is little and it has been so much of a long time. Several hundred pigs are out there sleeping on the porch that lines my rooms, culled in long pills of flubby bodies, at which I am the center rising. Floors for my house to the evening, covering the smell. Today the piggies' sound is fiber, turning puffy in the stun. My blood beneath my feet demands a crunchsong. It splatters around my knees.

I turn a second time to see the house here from the distance and the house as well is covered in my leakage. The cats are curdled in there, painting themselves onto the air around them by stench, by the fission of the heat going and coming through their skin. I have skin too. It is textured, false hamburger. I bite me to make sure that's true, and that I am.

Note to another: back face forward, I count the steps it takes to leave in sets of 26. One could make a list. Itemize. Alphabetize. Create a taxonomy with some allegorical significance, such as numbers, such as five. Such as the rattle of battle. For each set of 26 I extend one of my ten fingers. When I reach the tenth, I bite again. My arm renders the tickmarks on it like little crystals, a tattoo I made myself. In this way the system of 260 is not so hard to hold. I have to know how to get back here when I am done with wherever else there is. My flesh will make the map in return to counteract this accident of cells, the cluster of my honey and my arguments with mud. These never had, nor did they require, the blessing of the Church. They were never a part of Latin or Roman law, but had been prevalent in the underlying Celtic and Saxon cultures. A priori.

Animals conceal the location of their den or nest from predators. A posteriori. Humans attempt to consciously conceal aspects of themselves from others due to shame, or from fear of violence, rejection, harassment, loss of acceptance, or loss of employment.

Note to another: being the one more than on all fours. Difference in a nutshell. Sharing being one way for men to establish traditional relations with other men. In a cap. Soft, with a pom. Melted, with a thrust. In many places this change was seen as radical, and was met with great doubts about its effectiveness. Proved neat with a knife.

Secret societies.

My blood rises.
My blood rises.
My blood rises toward a long blot, the time-system of the city left unnamed, which in its evening spackle would click so loud some nights I could no longer feel my teeth inside my head. The god arms of its machine spins long before me, making whorls. I can see that it was not even really there, and yet I saw that it was there.

Organizations conceal nefarious behavior, secret 'laws' are initially secret. Secret societies use secrecy as a way to attract members by creating a sense of importance. Too, society.

My blood rises.
My blood rises.
My blood rises to cross the ocean of blue sand having risen over where the ghetto met the lofts, all our skin having clogged up so deeply in such acceleration more are buried than survived. More cats gather on the sand's face, a wilder breed than those around my house. As they sense me passing, on my stairwell, overhead, they claw and rasp and suck themselves. In the sand they shit and dig up strands of hair that lead to heads. Inside of which, fruit. Inside of which, ways.

Secret societies.

Never remember. If one can leave anything, one would leave that. Like that which one cannot. Cannot not. Well, one can. One chooses not to. To not not to. That is the taxing power. The authority *of*. Here. Proof of naked dogmatism. Excitement, mean. Ejaculation. Speech, say again. Again. Acts of jurisprudence. Of justice. The bone-chilling kind. Preservation is one of the goals of information security. Techniques used include physical security and cryptography. The jury was something else. It didn't represent God, but rather twelve or more individuals who, like as not, would fail to come up with the solution God would want. Wanting nothing. The latter depends on the secrecy of cryptographic keys, is central to organized crime. Too, there are the souls of others. No feeding, not at this time. One must remain, must never say. The tough cases which had no resolution (just as today) could easily be mocked by the public, if the decision by the jury was inconclusive, or not in agreement with all the facts, or emotions of the populace.

My blood rises.
My blood rises.
My blood rises with a tremble I've not known, pouring thinner as my veins grew dry unto turpentine. And yet I have such beat inside me. I make more. I think I make more.

My blood has wide steps and no railings. Its blue face is my mind hole. My heartbeat murmurs in it saying words I've said again. Governments often attempt to conceal information from other governments and the public, including weapon designs, military plans, diplomatic negotiation tactics, and that obtained illicitly from others ('intelligence'). Most nations classify material according to the level of protection needed (hence the term 'classified information').

Secret societies.

I walk forward upon my blood stairwell to a landing made of ice. The ice feels soft under my fingers, also a jelly, and yet it holds me up. My blood continues around the structure searching for whereon to move in, slicking the face of the gleamcube. Through the skin of ice all white from cracking, I can see a body centered in the frame—a person, rendered full on, held horizontal, nude. The thick of the ice obscures the facial structure and the specifics of the flabby form but for a brandmark on the chest. The brand is in the shape of a star, I think, or asterisk, what's the difference, its tines a slight shade darker than the night.

The cube is melting, or intends to.

I look back toward from where I came—my old held house on the horizon, fuming with the gust of southern wind. My blood by now has borne to form around it, a fist or organ, in which now there is no door.

The wet runs off the cube's face going blubby the more I walk. My blood, leading back down to the brown gash of the rooms where I have lived these years, still stands, though when I try to move to put my foot back on it my foot goes fully through.

Through the ice I see the body rising to me, surfacing as the ice thins. As it comes, I can see more of what about it: the hulk of meat around the jaws from incensed chewing; the bone spurs welling up around the neck; the countless pierced nipples, like mine; the gold jewel of the navel; the thicket of pubic hair, braided to disallow any exit or entry, adorned with barrettes; the knees, raw from such rubbing; nails grown long as emery boards. He or she has as well my same colors eyes, I think. Through the ice, I can see the mouth is moving saying something.

[•]

Never mind. Pretend one said nothing.

There's a grammar at work here, it should be noted, wearing the coveralls with a banker's bottom, all confusion in the manner *of*. Mustn't say which way.

Stop it.

I do not aim to hear.

I do not need to know to need to where to have the why or when.

Stop it.

I look around. The stairs are flustered, humming up with tsetse flies: little pills pushed out of the spoils of my aorta. My house is being brown: rounder than a potato, with tines that act like arms, reaching out for any instant, any birds caught in its warm. I am sinking. The body underneath me becoming more and more the floor. The helmet on my head going bananas, as well as any other fruit. My blood by now a cylinder around me, surreptitious in its scary, rising up new walls without the windows covering the sky. The ice floor gone enough now to be fully flesh: my body double underneath me, wheezing, learning to sit up in the hurt, sit straight up into my ass, my back, my cheeks, my duodenum, my earlobes, my frontal lobe, my gristle, my hives, my ideas, my jugular, my kidneys, my loving lips, my mouth, my mind…

Stop it.

Must remember this: this. Government officials sometimes leak information they are supposed to keep. Or: that. Some states take an entirely different approach to discovery. Note that discovery in the United States is unique compared to other common law countries. Remember this: in the United States, discovery is mostly performed by the litigating parties themselves, with relatively minimal judicial oversight. The Federal Rules of Civil Procedure guide discovery in the U.S. federal court system. Many states have adopted discovery procedures based on the federal system; some closely adhere to the federal model, others not so closely. By the Fifteenth Century, the law had become corrupted, and was only another weapon, along with physical violence, for the unscrupulous to achieve their ends.

When it sits inside the blood room we are two of us, both one. We are looking hard into one another. There could be a coil, just there, where sat number eight. Pick one. Three? Alternately, election is a growing issue, particularly vote counts on computerized vote counting machines. The body double's size is rolled. The hair over the genitals give smoke off when I rub. While voting, citizens are acting in a unique sovereign or 'owner' capacity (instead of being a subject of the laws, as is true outside of elections) in selecting their government servants.

Stop it.

One remembers that like it was yesterday. It is argued that it is impermissible as against the public in the area of elections where the government gets all of its power and taxing authority. Was it yesterday? It is argued that it is permissible as in the public in the area of ejections where the governed gets all of its taxing and author-function. Ratify, as the family would say when fishing. In any event, permissible varies significantly with the context involved. They remained a local and obscure phenomena. One of a kind, it was, its chin receded in the manner *of*, quite nicely. It had forgotten to shave along the tip of the neck, just where it's pointed, and this made one love it all the more, for it needed, it was clear, to forget. An alpine sweater, perhaps. Love during wartime. The lap lap lap of indiscretion along the base.

I look and roll within my helmet, looking for where the two of us can meet our eyes. His or her eyes are big and bubbling, each thin slipped sphere shape rising from her pupil to the lid, popping against the peel of his or her lens there, right then left then right. From the nostrils too there pours a new translucent liquid gushing back down into the mouth—a conduit of feeding. I cock my thumb to taste the run and get a buzzing where the flesh hits. In my mouth, regardless, sound makes snow, the peel of acid and TV polish giving little spark reams up my front. A warble. I drink another. I feed what I can feed.

When his or her mouth is overflowing with the goo stuff, despite my helping out, the body begins to talk for real. I can hardly hear him or her here through my helmet, and for the rising of the land, as somewhere beyond the slow room of my own blood above my ex-house on the melted-away floor, I can see down into the cat fluff where the putty has turned hard, and everything is rising in the heat of coming day. Underneath the lip I can hear a second screaming in the first speech, a heedless joke made of all wind, with which the air for years has cut the rock and floors and roofs and streets and stone plates into consecrated veins, holes where our people pour their money to see what god or we have made.

[•]

When one was younger, as one must have been, one can't always have been here, now, or at least there're rumors to the contrary, or at least there's a say-so, for one could tell other stories, stories which would quite definitely place one in other places, with an entirely, that is to say, a partially different perspective and one's hair would be otherwise parted and one's teeth somewhat better, more of them, for example, or more indigenous, at any rate.

At one point in history some exchanged these things, or rather these sets of things, for others not of their kind. Always, that is to say. One may be a victim of 'guilt complex,' but this invokes another kind of analysis. More internal, more judicial. Trial by ordeal or battle avoided these problems. The result in difficult cases was almost always clear cut. Judges didn't have to make tough decisions, didn't have to make, didn't have to make tough decisions. This, in retrospect, seemed misguided. Though it should be noted that if one avoided retrospection, things would right themselves straight off. There's a museum for that, as is recollected, history being particularly amenable to the glass case and the white wall. And if one squeezes at the bottom, a plop of art. In the blood, under a new skin, I strum a fifteen hundred stringed guitar. My hands choke notes out of dead wood and metal wide as fifty of me, loud enough to cover over any sort of voice. In the meat around my chest I hear me speaking, but I cannot make out the words, nor do I know at all the impulse. Busted lips. Potato grease. A glisten at the round of listening windows implanted in this second room, buried somewhere far enough the Astroturf and money that my finger phone will not dial out.

Through the glass the second surface still awaits, the mustard colored liquid having poured in high enough to obscure any air. Its color matches the twin holes punked in the blubber underneath my jaw. Wrappers of blue food nested in the bed burrow rat babies clean to nuzzle me at night. When I am the most tired I put one's sore head in my mouth to listen to it reek, the stink in speaking the transistors the length of cord by which its lungs attach to its tongue. It shits in my lap and I am laughing. My light is mayonnaise. My life is knocking gauge marks along my rectum, which in the night, I know, from the sleep-screaming, allow pears of our new religion in.

A poster of a black bear just above me watches what I eat. I scratched its face off with my hangnail last night and waking up today it had grown back with bigger jaws. I stand up with the guitar and do my calisthenics, hulking noise out with the pressure of my pelvis and spine. The speakers in my cheeks. The bass woofer where my A is.

I am waiting for a door. For the bloodwaters to slush off again or rise so high there is no sight.

My double, through my fingers, plays another song I've never heard: some grog of eleven chords and buzzfuzz that stands the flesh up on my arms. My flat tits give me an erection. I watch my hands thicken on the strings, ripping blisters into soft days where I have done nothing but press buttons for the gift of cash. The button panel in this room all unlabeled, doing nothing but indent and click. I imagine a room somewhere where these impulses are fed.

From the bear's face, hours later, my pads so swelled I can hardly tell one from the next, the glow hole where the graphs come ejects another ream. The paper is moist, printed backwards, blue on blue.

HELLOWEAREINYOU

it says, in dilapidated electronic cursive.

EVERYHOURNOWISOURS

I fold the letter four ways by four ways by four ways again to make it tidy, slide it up inside me by the hole, as I've been told.

I look again at the print out, it looks different, other words where I read words. Then, a map—a shape of money—a postcard—an image of a gold tree—the image shifting every time I blink and I cannot find a way to never blink.

Sometime last I look again and see the picture is of me. In the picture I am standing beside a picture of myself. The other me has money in my hands. A telephone around the neck and a smile as wide as our whole face, and so much younger than I ever. A clean sheen to the teeth. A more black hairdo. No rings.

The me inside the picture looks like me, palms empty.

I try to kiss me in the picture and my scrunching makes me blink and when I see again the paper's black. Burnt or browned out. Smudgy. The paper tastes like ice.

I go to the sleeping sandpile underneath the blackbear and shake through it with my fingers to find the string, its butt end on this side tied to a washer big as my fist. The washer shocks me when a touch it, a reminder of the light, and therefore, by inverse, the cut of closets, my insides. I pull the string length by length wrapping my fist into a glove. Around my meat the string makes me hear singing through the helmet an ecstatic ring of bright. Against my chest, taped with the tape paste, the guitar sings with it, scrubbing my ribcage and nipples with the butter of its nowhere croak, the power eating through my chest. I pull and pull, causing the backbeat of my snapping muscles, cells burning as the string around my fingers winds thick. Through the glassy walls the liquid runnels, forming patterns on the mash; our city like the night enclosed around egg. Someone is looking down another tunnel with a fat eye.

From the sandpile, I pull the sheet. My mirror. Glow dementer. The object of no shell. It has been mandated out of sight by now for longer than the house stood, than my hair's length, than the new cut of my chin. The tattoo along my inner right nostril, a reminder enforced by our State's men. Secret societies. The last database confession from my father sewn into the black tag of my shirt, where it burns: 1215.

Each time I think of which I must shriek out of me in slur, my voice crashed in color like the white of rotting raw bacon on the sand-freed mirror's face. 1215. My sound jumbles the grain along the sternum of it showering the cell's floor. 1215. I stand above the mirror checking my gums and tissue. I feel it try to read my mind again. 1215.

1215 was also the year of the Magna Carta. Inevitable. That's retrospect. That's belief. That's bitterness, and then relief. That's the stuff. Among other things, it limited the Courts of Eyre. Purposely not made available to the general public and hence to any enemy by the military in order to gain an advantage or to not reveal a weakness, avoid embarrassment or to help in propaganda efforts. These were circuit riding courts of the King which were roundly feared and hated. Those may be found also in the square, or in a landscape. Unpeopled. Unstaring. A transplant, even if rejected, alters the organism from within. Military in nature such as the strengths and weaknesses of weapons systems, tactics, training methods, number and location of specific weapons and plans, they had a reputation for being imperious and angry. If kept, a permanent mark of the present absent, the nongenerative regen. Come again. Say again. Again.

Another message from the glow hole:

HURRY UP

I lay the guitar face down on the floor.

In the flashcut off the surface, flat beneath me I straddle my image with my width, my legs in towers rising from points left and right beside the mirror up to a cruxpoint where my gut goes. My meat is big and bumpy where my clothing, as I remove it, bends, the creaseworn rummage of my tummy and my white thighs fuddled in a mass of chunk and hair. In me I can feel me. I rub my bulging with my thumb searching the crease for softer spots. Certain sections of me crunch a lot. My birthmark sticking gently to my fingers. The blood around the room against the windows going whorled with this fantastic darkness.

The blackbear watches while I work.

In the me inside the image I cannot find the cash. I cannot find the will to smile or how I'm younger. I cannot find the telephone. Through my stomach skin I feel pebbles hidden. A goo lump. Something stone. In my image, below, my stretchmarks as well appear reflective, bouncing back and forth with lettuced light in pins. At certain angles my bulge will disappear. I rub and rub. I'm rashing up. The blackbear seems to smirk. The blood around the windows changing colors: blue, then other blue, then other blue, then a damaged blurb of purple, red, redder, reddest, white, whiter white, a blue more blue than blue, unto a red more red than was ever, unto black. The wobble of it throbbing. The glass as if to smile itself, stirring cracks up along its inseam in the image of my flesh. The mirror darker now, in league around me, my me there more beautiful, more old. I can't see me but me reflected. The printer behind me squirting more words for anyone. My hand way up in my gut. I'm reaching. Somewhere in there, somewhat.

In the glass I watch my eyes go glossy while inside my fold I feel my fingers find some hold. A hard handle at my sternum sections. As I take grip, the room makes spin moves. The blackbear above me barking and liquid dripping from its teeth. So far in me, I pull my handle, and in my flesh of head, I match the room, the two kinds of spinning making one move of them. Equal. Sitting. The room upon the room.

Through my throat, then, there goes a bang. Some rim of scummy squiggle beeped.

Out of my mouth I spit a bell. The bell bursts out of my lips and booms against the ground. It rings a little and is still. I lean to pick it up, still inside me holding the handle in my flesh too. My leaning body leaves the mirror, no longer doubled, my torso absent of my head. Outside the frame, using my free hand, I shake and shake and shake the bell shape, as does my other, I imagine, beyond the other frame, and neither one makes sound. I shake it hard. I shake. I shake it. I shake until…

Out of the bell's mouth there falls a blue gift.

Inside the gift there is a gun.

Inside me the handle begins vibrating, coming loose around the edges. Curly. My hot fist in me spreads, lifting in my bloodstream where the blood is growing back. My hand comes out the color of a dowel rod. The glassy walls ring where the bell would not. Through the seam I hear voices yards off from my bloodroom booing and making faces, fingernails on something else. I wipe my hand off on my shirt. The smudgemark is a diamond, isn't it?

With my free hand, I take the gun. In one hand, it, one hand the bell. They weigh both mostly the same. I ring the gun with one hand. I shoot the bell into the air. I put the bell into my mouth. The metal rim is larger around my mouth's hole, stretching at my lip. My trigger finger sweats. I rub the brass around the bell lip counting its ridges. One ridge. A language. Overhead the gun makes music, its only note. Again. Again.

This noise.

Against the ground in reverberation with the banging my guitar murmurs up more notes to go along, the strings singing on the impacted floor of blood. The guitar walks across the floor, its necked head jagging forward on the mush until it hits into the wall and stabs its glass face once, skitters back, stabs it again. The warbling of the sound lets the guitar stab the wall over and over. It perforates around the room, a slow leak opening for the dark fluid to come pouring back in at me again. The slick around my feet. The gun intoning. The bell's mouth warm at my mouth. I think to kiss it. I tongue the bell's pendulum, lick its clapper, the bulb of it shaped the same way as my cell. The gun now gushing liquid when I blip the trigger. The liquid pouring in.

I take the bell out of my mouth. The ring around where it had fit me leaves a wider hole. My teeth ache. I am hungered, halved in halves of half. In gloves of glowing, where my arm still stands slick from where it went inside me, and my other mirrored arm below. The mirrored me still looking at me all this time. My eyes rung with the bells shape in the pupils, new matching tattoos on either cheek. The wet around me lapping and in the mirror rising to cover up my feet around my knees. The guitar underwater pops and pops.

I put the gun into my mouth where the bell was, my newly glistened gap. I watch my double do the same beneath me. I see it grinning. I watch my two arms ring the bell again. The sound shakes out an egg. The egg breaks where I touch it and from its shape births two more eggs, each of which break and birth up three eggs. The eggs sink underneath me in the liquid, still replicating as they descend and thickening the wet, the glass from guitars and eggs and pressure puckering the glass walls of the blood room, my bloating room, our room, foam. Somewhere out there now the voices louder. My house of voices under sleet. This pupa I've cemented, already breaking on the air. I shake the bell again, both bells, and eggs are slewing, plopping from my hand. I cannot get my hand off the bell. Eggs. Eggs. More shaking. Each egg splitting into kids. The printer behind me screaming, wrapping words around my legs, climbing up the kneecaps, pockmarks, puddles of me where my skin has yet to burst.

WHAT ARE YOU DOING UP HERE

WHERE DO YOU THINK YOU'RE GOING

OPEN

THIS IS MY HOUSE, IN NO HOURS

GIVE ME YOUR OTHER ARM

I shake the words off and I say no. The gun between my teeth is mealy, made of bunny goo. I bite and pinch its muzzle closed, folded in half. I pull the trigger. I hear the gushing liquid, adding back into my blood. I give off smoke through both my eyes. The guff of it rising overhead me.

From the mirror, too, the smoke comes poured. And through the new holes in the glass face. And from the boiling of the mess of eggs and eggs and eggs and the guitar: the strings and shells beneath me clinging to wet which clings to me which clings to where I am, making new skin, clustering like ice. I feel an urge to lie in hair. I tongue the muzzle back into a hole, off-shaped, as am I.

I shoot myself, and me too, in the center of our mouths.

There is a bite. The smoke is silent. Some strings sing nothing. Eggs around my crown. My blood is coming through the glass now. My blood is massive. The floors are stolen from my feet, the paper of the blurt doing a making, having me to hold. The mirror pressed against me, my form adhering to the ripped skin of my chest. My doubled eyes doing the blink the blink, pressing wet on wet and the new wet coming for them, to seize over the sight, eggs, to wrap around the building, blood, to return me to where I thought I was before I was there.

[•]

There is a collection of dream homes, one can find them in books, or ask friends, whatever one's got, one is not one to point fingers or name names, but there they are, primarily elaborate, full, that is to say, of rooms and other rooms, and people who bear an uncanny resemblance to some mother. One had a dream house once, as may be recalled, but it was only a façade.

[•]

Unmaking. That's the thing of it, history in the unmade. See how easy. Not to be. Not not. Others by others, others sought in others. Nearly 2500 years ago, so-and-so wrote, 'Do nothing; for Time sees and hears all things, and discloses all.' Not written, said. Saying is something. Never say. Say three hundred and fifty-nine. Say a silver case. Of what kind. The promulgation of the jury system required the taking of testimony from witnesses. This led to growing use of writs compelling attendance at trials, using the clause 'sub poena'. So one who wishes to see—what was it? Sight itself. No. Along the walls and down the horrid doors. No. Unsonorous. Nothing unisonous. Vision. See vision. That's it. The question inevitably arises: Did the writ subpoena develop in the Court of Eyre, or in the Court of Chancery? The thing to be said exactly. That tooth. Perfect whole in the middle. Mustn't say whole. Hole either. Too simple, that. Must see it, the thing to be said exactly, it, in its particulars. Minute. Small relatively speaking. Poll shows a inchish surge for particulars. Itch, that is to say. Make a run for it. Fail. Fail again. Say again. Again. And then another agenda. As if it were yesterday. And why not. No matter. No difference. All difference. No matter. Organized as such. See how easy. Not to be. Not not. There were writs of a somewhat similar nature to be found in both courts. Swearing it, it so. O difference. Two, for looking. Plus something very nearly a flipper. Pair of flippers. Pair of unscissors. Bills (writs of complaints) were the method by which a litigant could make a story known in the courts of the 13th and 14th century England. Because novel fact patterns frequently emerged, there was a tendency to become creative in the writing of bills of complaint and writs. Fiend of righteousness. Never mind. Pretend one said nothing. Mustn't say, that is to say. Say what to do: remember. I appear wrapped up in the rope again. The helmet closer to my skull and drool filling the gaps.

Through the glass the room is awkward. Smear marks on the wall where I had tried to make my body gather up. The blur of blood of me no longer looks like anything or body. That blood inside me still, pummeling the outline. Wanting.

The upstairs has been sealed. Blocked off with panes of glass of plastic that will not allow me back. My hands behind me. Ass behind me.

Another hour in today. Another long loop of the slow bone in me creaking age into its center.

I hear me standing behind me also, where the air is. I hear me open up a drawer. Put something in it. Close the drawer. The wall of the room is so long I cannot turn around. I feel the fingers grip the helmet, adjust buttons. No one says my name.

I am lifted half inside me to stand again and stoop toward the door. Across the wall, a tiny window where the sky again has been removed. Again has been remaindered to something softer than I am. One day I could walk into it. One day, some direction, some long sway of fabrics days are made of.

Through the Food Chute the light comes clean. I put my mouth around the spigot, drink up what I can suffer, though the long mouth groove of the helmet aligned above my ear. Hear me behind me grunting as I taste the sun juice. It runs in needling thickets down the fatfolds of my neck, splitting into rivulets and runnels again turning to bumps there and also soaking in my shirt. Through my shirt my nipples gleam a little, and give some juice, too, though there is nothing there to feed.

Halfwet and followed, I am rolled along the unlit hallway with the windows out onto the realm. I try to look along the pane in one way or another to catch a fraction of someone there but can't or cannot or will not or won't. My helmet stays hard and spinny, a bit of something caught rolling in the bulb, a roach or loose change around my head case aggravating in and out. My arms burn on the carpet. In the spin I still cannot make out a face, my other me there beside me. The light is, all here, ice.

Through the one spot that looks into the garage I see the garage has been pulped full, the magazines I'd asked for already shredded by my other there behind. No distraction. No division. No shiny images of tits and cash. No turning on the TV knowing when or who or how long, but subject to the creation of a gash.

Two bulldozers in the backyard are in time together playing Bash The Ground. The extra workers stand there watching, placing bets and eating dog. Two more dogs hung on thick black rotisserie spits over the sandpit where a mound rises from the earth. The grass and other growths around it appear stunted, the moss encaving on itself and blacking in. In the gap of seconds of my rolling passing I see the smaller of the two dozers hit a tree, and from the tree bursts up a goldenrod bouquet of fat and runny snow. Among the snow the men are jeering, their mouths open. They are inhaling all our sky. Two of the men are naked, two are hungry, two tattooed so black across their face they have no lines. In here, on me, my two old blue marks in the crease between my pointer finger and my thumb. Two of them tremble in the ring around my belly. Two of anything. No names.

Down the hall I see the other room. I can't remember what the room is for. I feel me stick me in the center of my back with something sharp to cure more blood out, another new door, another way. I'm sneezing. My arms are heavy. Something spilling out of my back: a pour like lather, no, lightning, no, writing. No. I can't remember what the room is for.

In the roll I slow time and look up. I see the hall again, hear me below me in the floor. I say a lot of words at once. They come out of me onto my hands and wear me. A machine hits the house from outside. The workers cheer. The roof in leak again, my leaking hole again.

Forward again, back to rolling. I make my hands into two new suns, shaped fists full of heat and burning at my meat. I swing wide in dragging to punch the two walls on either side but cannot under the ropes wrapped around me like a skin that no one grew for. In the wanting I make moan shapes. Bubble pop against my roofmouth. I can hear me behind me choke a laugh, trying not to light my mind with presents. Trying not to not to not.

I am not supposed to know about me but I know about me, in the evenings, every night. The way my skin pops up in tents with something underneath it and more lashing of my tongue. And the bleeding. And the bleeding. The size inside my walls.

[•]

Through the last window of the many along the far side of the hall, the last thing I see of those men working is the hulk of white they pull up from underground. I only catch a clasp of it, but it is bigger than the largest person I have seen, and it has eyes like someone else's, and it is all over the ground. The men begin to gather round, raising their fists, taking knees, becoming...

Organized as such. Spotted as a snowy sky. Who keeps they eye open to the falling. Brooder. Director. The external implementation, reiteration, regurgitation of something something. Say again. Never say. Against this novelty, was a strong reaction, wanting to keep the number of writs to a minimum. Copies attached. No originals. A thin line down the side, such as might be found in a well. O well. One remembered a kind of smile, thin and rigorous, set in a sort of virtue smacked in the mouth by a kind of benevolence. That would be fine.

Then there is only, again, the wall. And I know I cannot stop myself from moving. And I know I will not go back. Now or ever, not in this house, in this licked length and rasp of skin. I run along the wall, shoulder just brushing, the cells between me and what I cannot see, and in my being seen unseen. And in the cusp of just behind me, which by gods fucked fucking flapping gap of gods' rooms, I can feel. Can feel you right there with the ribcage and the paste puff and my image in a clasp. Can feel him pushing where the ropes are bunched least. Feel her with the screwdriver in the night, tightening the helmet and laughing at me and making candy out of everything I've given, what I've coughed up. What I needed.

With my blood flowing in your blood where you were just behind you also, where someone is behind you, too.

Don't look. You can't look either. If you do you will not see. You will not eat the thing you wanted no matter how far down it goes inside your mouth. An example is seen from the time of Edward II of England: in 1310–1311 John Soke, a litigant appeared in person before the Common

Bench, exclaiming in great frustration, 'For God's sake, can I have a writ to attaint this fraud?' Judge Stanton replied, 'Make your bill and you shall have what the court can allow.' Or at least one had one very nearly like it once before. A kindness. An inner presence. Pomp, like so many small dogs. One of another. Murdered, idem. Still, there's something to be said for mothers. Numbers, mean. Aggregation. Accumulation. Line them up along the walls and down the horrid doors. This illustrates the great flexibility of the writing of writs to conform to the changing fact situations as they varied from case to case. Killing through accommodation.

Juxtapose.

Ring the bell until there is no answer. Then analyze. It is an occupation, that thing that is something inside. That sense of permanence. Some call it peace. Restful. Rester. Toothless. Bloated. Upstairs. At that time, a plaintiff who sued by bill was not liable to fail for defects in the form of a bill, provided the bill told an intelligible and consistent story. There were many once, like kittens. Like eating. Again. For another day. Though can never remember if it's the day one is eating for, or the day before. Try eating for the day after. That would be a good joke on the mustn't-say. The act of leaving through unofficial or illegal ways.

On this hall, as I'm rolling, the rope's not rope but more of my blood, pilling off of me along the long way of the house inside the house, where as the walls continue to show none, and the windows there behind me showing anybody who would be there, and I cannot: rolling blood off of me, skin off of me, me off of me: me above: me above me taking what I give off and making making making more house, more other self, more other me, more nothing, while outside the men and the machines destroy. Rolling farther, hotter, faster, master: rolling making semicolons out of every each twin bruise. My diction picking. My eyeholes glowing: light on light where as I roll and roll I become thinner, I find, inside this house, and me above me, on this hall the floor goes down: the hall not curving as it had the last time I could remember having gone along it, to the far end, but in the manner of an off ramp aiming down.

Pomp, did one mention? Yes, recently. As in recently ate, or eating. Chewing, swallowing, swallowing, chewing. In that order. History, as previously mentioned. Said again. Smooth the hair, iron the scars on the shoulders. One must make something of oneself. Fruition. Faith. That's the stuff. As a matter of procedure, the judge would question the plaintiff in order to bring out the cause of the complaint. Once this was accomplished, the subsequent proceeding under the bill would be carried out as if there was a legitimate writ. One remembers, and this can be said without fear of rigor, a weekend involving only that which could be got in the here and now, the here and how. One is entirely local. A call. Someone's neighbor. A wall. One is sure of this, for there have been seen the signs of occupation. Signs in another language. All other languages. Things said more imperatively than other things.

This hall, I felt, goes down under the house. I see now, seeing the sizing of it, widened as the stirrup hits the lip. I barely miss to bop my head hard on the lip of where in the house there was the door, the downgrade of our level leaving some dumb inch for every step. Down down, and that behind me right there for every more. I rub the floor, its holding half becoming there above me instead a ceiling, pink underbellied, ripped and ripped with all the years above where we had walked. Popping pudmarks where things had leaked through and the friction and the spilling and the sound. I can hardly keep my mouth from hulking pulp and muscle. I spit up a little dinner on my bib. I try to hold the grown rotation of my head around my head again again inside the helmet, nothing, not even no one, rope on rope. The slick slope of the floor becomes more steep for every shoulder I'm turned over. It rattles down and down and down, an inverse for my stairwell, and yet still cauldroned of my blood. My veins unsaying every worst lurch here spinning again.

Unsaid. Say again.

By the 15th century, the bill would typically pray that a subpoena should be issued to secure the appearance and examination of the defendant. This is the difference between descriptive and normative cultures. Differences, it should be said. Ambition, for one. The coat-buttons, or those things that look like coat-buttons, are much larger, for another. Thought about saying this was the difference between philosophy and history. Might still say it, but save it for later. Something about particulars. Something about having been said. About having been not said, about having been said by another. The rest is there. Everywhere. Walls, floors, ceiling. At least what one assumes are walls, floor, ceiling, though one has been known to be wrong on any and all points. Matter of geography and calculation. Matter not of history. Just like father. Not that father, the other one. The one without the umbrella. The one that lies elsewhere. Poof! Love unlost. A matter of punctuation. Of being told what to do and when. Another kind of saying, to be sure. Mustn't say. The terms not used in law. Take in the aggregate. Then subtract. Him. Always him. Never him. Gone and good. Puts one in mind of history. Perfect wholes. Disregard the remainders. Also a criminal offense in many places, and it is likely to result in time being added to, as well as being placed under. Perhaps some fried potatoes. Perhaps with mayonnaise. As if had teeth, as if had tongue. *Je commences de parler*. Say. *Les frites avec de la mayo*, as the normative might have said. Should make a list of what might be said, alphabetized. Color-coded. All in red. Which red. That one. After a forensic analysis. After an aria. Inside a chemise. Outside assistance. The source of the word writ, or writ subpoena has been ambiguous. Friends or relatives arrange for items to be smuggled into. For instance, a fake gun smuggled in, used to threaten and disarm. Works like a charm. Such as the other day. Or, arrange to have a standing by, ready to receive outside the compound. Because mail, gifts and communications are usually monitored, it can be difficult to ensure this sort of assistance. Inside assistance. Most require assistance inside; usually from, but it's possible to, typically through turning a blind eye. 'Anomalies' or sabotage. Deaf ear. Unvest. Unsaid. Say again.

[•]

Where I land my hair is wheat.

The floor beneath the house is purple, ageless and so old. The walls are ash muddled with money and a squeezing sense of mayonnaise, and yet not really there at all at all as when I look again there is just air, the floor beneath it spreading out into a nothing rubbing cold in vision on my teeth. My ropes where days had gone on, my sweat and giggling poured into their tines, have rolled off in my downhill rattle, or are otherwise removed.

The Statute of Westminster II (1285) under the section *in consimili casu* (in similar case), attempted to limit the number of writs that could be issued. This naturally caused a fit of laughter in oneself and can still set some to shaking.

Some days there are no days in the days where days are days and days are done. Dumb dicklicked days of backtalk, my mouth and someone else's together purred. These are the times that seem most allegorical, stuffed with. One meant to emphasize that. W*ith*. There. Done. Like fashion, or like in a fashion. It's all in the wearing. In the mode of another preposition, another comma, another comment. In some jurisdictions, it is a criminal offense. The punishment depends on whether using force or violence or setting fire; the philosophy of the law holds that it is nature to want. To absent. For instance, those who do not break any other laws are not charged for anything and no extra time is added; however, officers are allowed to shoot those attempting. It is illegal if violence is used. Nothing doing. As an example, from 1221 there is the case of Thomas de la Hethe. He had been presented by the grand jury with an indictment accusing him of being an associate of a notorious felon named Howe Golightly. Thomas refused to put himself on the country (accept a jury trial). One doesn't trust the other anymore. One doesn't trust the other one. Notwithstanding this refusal, the court declined to permit him any sort of trial by ordeal, but realizing the gravity of the situation they empanelled an impressive jury of twenty-four knights. These found Thomas guilty, and therefore he was hanged. Practice makes perfect, in other words. And in this way, one might ask that particular attention be paid to the conditional, the anxious tense that makes a winter coat such an abstraction. Being so much hope, not unlike the concept of history, as previously noted.

A tongue underneath my tongue here wants the water while my own tongue needs the waste of the same: the output of someone else poured off into me, pissbottles, whips and panties, letting and having, rip and rip. And rip! A ring through each and every tip bit of my nipples, weaving one bright and multicolored field. A branding on my sternum in the profile shape of someone's dad, or someone other than that, with large nostrils, portals to the mind.

To be compared with derisive laughter. The derisive laughter to be compared with an allegorical consideration. The allegorical consideration to be compared with the empty experience. The empty experience to be compared with the stereotypical motif. The stereotypical motif to be compared to the middle of the century, a time when key figures abound in true behavior.

Around my head the helmet has been switched out for a new one, lined with two way mirrors, through which I can see the room as any day—though underneath the house is not a room or house at all but more air than I've ever had inside me over any long amount of time. Rocks and putty, or trees and lighting. The men have left with their machines—or is that them I can hear shudder through the nothing, through the tent poles and the wire and my skin coming off in shower, as it seems the heat here needs to know me, wants to lift me up and see?

The sky here underneath the house is quite brown also, as is my upchuck, which has dried hard along my clothes into a new clothes, a uniform of long-held grease. A horizon in all directions wider than any night should be. In the center of it, one burned black dot, my house, watching as I am. The flood of floor no longer clearly set to say how I could have ever come down from it, or could get back, or where another want had been.

One might make a story about this, something shaped like a fish, with a small beginning, a longer and wider middle, and a quick end. Another example comes from the same year, 1221. An indictment indicated that the carcass of a stolen cow was discovered in William's shed. William did not express a claim to any particular sort of trial. He did state that the cow had been placed there by his lord, so that the latter could get his land as an escheat for felony. The serjeant who arrested William stated that the lord's wife had arranged for his arrest. In such a case, the court simply asked the indictors for more information. They related the whole story; William was acquitted by the court and the lord was committed to gaol (jail).

Underneath my house the road is all my blood forever and goes forward in a spindling brook, the flesh of earth around it making stem along in its summed someway forever heading on.

I believe I am no longer behind me as there is nothing left of me to feel. I do not even turn to see where I am not now, as I know and know I know, etc. And anyway, the new helmet is so heavy. And anyway, I see already how there is someone other there ahead... how there is someone other up there, along the hard tack of this land under the land. A fleshy body held in profile with the backmask of, what, a buried sun. Certain spindles of the squalling light around the figure make it appear larger and semi-fuzzed around the edge. I can tell the person or whatever is saying something by the bubble of its back, the spine bent slightly forward, the fomenting mouth. Otherwise the figure is stock-still.

And yet, as I approach it, first in slowing, along the long path of no path at all in so much light, with dimension of equal blank in all directions—a flattened plane of field, if adorned here and there with shapes of far off buildings, and the strewing of crap and garbage—the body does not grow any further close. Though it does not appear to move its arms or legs, assuming any inch or way at all, and no matter how hard or fast inside me I mush for moving forward I cannot make the body come. Cannot scrunch the lens of it against me any warmer or incoming or quite there, though the texture of the flat and funny sky rolls anyway, and my body licked by wind of going, and some vibration on the air is, while overhead the house in hole grows further away until it is no longer a portion of the sky but just a dot, then not at all.

I walk along the slim curve of the something going glowing with the heat in incandescence on my caked-in skin. The ground under my feet staying right there to fit the cupping of a series of cylinders embedded in the ground from which I step and step on forward on the soft mush as if designated to be underneath a deity. All directions coming going. The figure only ever there ahead. Sometimes, in the glare off the mirrors, I see the crease of my forehead there appeared, the roasting redmash of my faceskin growing burny in the bright where I am aiming to walk, my pupils somewhat centered with separate minor figures at their heart of heart of ash, I think it is, also watching without moving, I think, at a fixed distance in my skull. Their outlines do not match the outline of the someone therefore far ahead, our split dimensions, a panorama curlicue split and splitting at the center, above the fat of all or any lust.

The person way on up there becomes a cow becomes a day becomes a doorbell, becomes something with seven hands and seven eyes, becomes a house again like mine way up there so that between the sky and it there is a whir, there is a sound of ill condition in duplication that whips the skin up on my hands, welts like where babies bite you when they're hungry and make the blood pour for days then too. The person becomes a person again, then two of them, standing back to back and spine to spine. Their arms point up into the nothing. Their other arm reaches out to me. They have open in their soft hands a gift I would imagine taking into my mouth if I could reach it, which I want to, and I run. When I get tired of the running I fall over and when I can stand up again this time I walk.

I walk for all the hours I have in me on the furthering unfolded field. No rush of struggle allows toggle but for the map of overhead, which here induces sky to become hashmarked, to become bubbly and all wet, to become as charblack as the face of a never turned on TV. The face of the floor remains undaunted, laughing foot for foot for foot, and I am flat again, my nipples having sucked into my chest under the swelling of where the air here makes me burn. My piercings pock the strumming of me, marking each milk location on my chest with tone of gold. Along the walk, which walks on with me, I pull up on a ringlet here and there. I find under the lip of the earth the fat pink pocky of me there buried all throughout the terrain to the deadlight held up with my pinching fingers and from the meat of me I suck. Drink up the milk all muddled in me. I taste like Diet Coke and pills. Fuck. My helmet hurts around the hole for where my mouth is and buzzing hard around my tongue, the sensors in my ass squeaking for what I know I should not eat, fuck, for all the hours and the tables and the food I will be fed by will alone because I am, all other food removed in light of days here and the begging of the fly, the husk of gift of Senate removing need today, today, giving unto us the unburden of no decision, which I herein know I will not, and so must now, violate. I drink the fuck out of me. I really slurp it. I taste fast like what I always imaged the blue part of a fire might. I taste until I can't taste through all my throat's thick and lined like wallpapers piling thicknesses for dumb months unto dumb years on a wall, new bodies asking of the color for the hours they will be awake and look and look, and my color too within me shifting, and I am so full, strummed and stoned on my own beverage in the image of no baby, and I realize I am drooling, have become covered in my filth, my milk a dress and second lining and a map of where I've been in this short time, though looking back I see the trail goes on forever, purple milk on purple floor, and I am looking back so hard I can't see, and my head tucked underneath my ribs, and I pull hard to look back up and lick my lips and find the suck again, and I look up again and see no figure, no figure ever there, and in its place close up now is another machine, is a plow. One has no right to reason, or to be moved; this is what makes it Biblical. Though desire is often mistaken for duty, insofar as others are concerned.

[•]

This is the story of great love, of the non-song sung in the hole of the other. It was these that provided the gravest difficulties with jury trials following the abolition of trial by ordeal. Among us, we have another understanding. Between or among one, that is, as in or regarding the others, or that hypothetical audience one likes most frequently to address, are otherwise occupied with inflaming their sexual fantasies and saving truths. Or vice versa. In any event. Upon the calling of a general Court of Eyre, it was easy to assemble a thousand or more jurors, who could be questioned, and pronounce a prisoner guilty or not. In the preface, one must be sure to write about this. One could imagine something involving someone by whom one is deeply influenced. As in a masque, or a birthday party. Not him, though, as that would place the emphasis too precisely on a particular time of day, bypassing the twinge of the later hour. Still, if the proceedings were instigated upon the delivery and indictment from a gaol (jail), before a non-professional judge, most prisoners were coerced to put themselves upon the mercy of a jury trial, and forego their ancient right to trial by ordeal. One notes that one finds oneself most vital in one's particulars, and thus must avoid them like so many hazelnuts. Like hazelnuts, mean, or a vision of hazelnuts, noisette, to put a marginal gloss on it. One would also like to include some decorative illustrations noteable for their rigor and variable conviction. Things that look very much like. As one is always (en 'fait') concerned with equivalency, it is only a matter of time before the comparison, the fair comparison, is appreciated. But not by him. There's so much one cannot say about him. Like the laughter of children. Like the games of children. Like the ambition of children, all kept close to the circle and out in the open. Like the toys of children. Like the regulation of prostitution being the insistence on a kind of time-keeping or standing in single-file, as if there was a window. One might wish there was a window. Or a boat. Not necessarily out, that is, or even glass, if there could be such a thing, here, in the absence of excessive argumentation.

[•]

The plow, when I sit down on it, is already running.

The plow has always been on and will be on forever also, whether I am on the plow or not.

I ride the plow like I am fucking something that feels very good—back arched, hips out, seated, rolls rolled back in my head, helmet pulling my head back a little further, like having hair pulled, which is how I like to have it done.

Underneath and all around me, anyway, the plow bucks up clouds of sky-high smoke—smoke or dust or something dusty. It sits hard on the lungs. It makes a second helmet around my helmet for which I am thankful as you can never be too protected in any light.

I can't remember how I did not see the smoke before I sat down on the plow or what was around the plow back then, though I can remember standing there before it, and the wanting, all the walls up in my life.

I ride the plow like I've been somewhere sometime and I am headed back there now. Between the smoke or dust or what the shit that shit is and the helmet and the helmet's helmet and the extra light and my dumb eyes I can't see much of anything.

This is where fiction comes in, and the fish-shaped story. Reason for the boat, the plow. What an ordeal fishing is. Not to mention the stereotypical motif, although it is far too late for that. There is a plan. Down to the particulars. It worked once, and one is terribly certain it would work once again. Just the once. That's what the bloated form used to say, 'just the once.' It seemed to be said by way of reclamation, or distinction, one can't be sure. If they refused a jury trial, there was no option but to keep them in prison until they changed their mind. Under these circumstances, the jury became a new form of ordeal. The entire affair seemed ripe for analysis in the way of a kind of common ground, a lot, to be more precise, judging from its dimensions. The judges, in difficult cases ceased to be inquisitors, and simply came to accept the verdict of the jury. The accused was pronounced either 'guilty' or 'not guilty'. He once claimed to be a portrait of himself, and he was not wrong about that. There was something about him that seemed representational, if not figural, and if not representational, reproducible, and if not reproducible, at least capable of being had. She had him, and that involved another gesture altogether. A swarming flash of intellect, someone said, though they were talking to someone else, or about someone else. The metaphor is inexact. The hieroglyphs, non-specific. The difference between bleeding and bloody. This result soon came to be accepted with as little doubt, as much as the result of the hot iron or cold water was accepted a generation earlier. This may return one to the allegorical hillocks, on, one means to say, in the manner of looking around, or up, being beneath in one's perceptions, as such structures are commonly wrought above the head rather than in the neck or about the nether regions. Though one has no claim on cogency or the reflective attribution. Why once, when one was much older than one am now, one had the distinct impression, and one has never forgotten the feeling. At first, there was no compulsion to deem the actions of a jury with any more rationality than that of the ordeal. Not now. Maybe later. One will try again on the 14th. Say the 23rd. Say the morning. Sadly. The ordeal had shown God's judgment in the matter. Make a note. Make several. Strung into a song worth singing on a guitar and putting the toe and heel of the soft boot to and fro—it will be an utter embarrassment. That's a show of ambition. Utter embarrassment. In the hard lower case. The verdict of the jury, while not necessarily congruent with God's will, nonetheless, was inscrutable. Perhaps poetry, then. One could rhyme something with something else. One could break up my sentences with small ballpeen hammers or snap them in two like twigs. Like twigs. Like worms, that is, leaving them to crawl off in opposing directions. They bleed, you know. They really do. It's just immaterial to anyone, that is to say, *to*. Just as one is. Just as he is. Is not, that is. The problem here is that one suspects the other's paying attention, and attention, as one must know from one's earlier education, which one assume one had, as early education is as inescapable as later ignorance, though not quite as warm around the shoulders or lightly belted about the waist, is very dear indeed. Share, as the French would say. Typically generous, the French. They left one all one's hands and teeth. Things laying in between. A story should be told. One should tell a story.

The smoke becomes a curtain.

The smoke becomes a sash.

In the run of the drummed motor I hear people say my name. I hear the doors to other buildings open and people eating dinner with their families and their friends. I know inside the smoke there are the buildings and the people and with the plow I take them on. I thunder head on into the swirl of something, my miasma, which is a fancy way of saying what in the name of all that's what.

I ride on, blood hot, holes stuffed, blue.

There is a lever on the plow that goes two ways—backward and forward—but for the smoke I cannot tell which one is what, so for long times I'll go one way and then for fun or pleasure I'll switch it up.

A second little toggle makes the plow turn this or that way on the pivot but that toggle's mostly stuck. Only for pushing or tweaking hard in one way or the other and hoping hard or bitching at it or just ripping it so hard it seems to nearly come off in my hand, can I get, I think, the plow to turn even inches out of our ongoing way. Which shouldn't matter, cause I can't see, but still seems good or right or necessary to keep doing, or at least I do it anyway.

There is no on or off button on the plow that I can feel.

I ride on saying everything aloud I always wanted and getting it exactly right now right, though there is no one here to hear it and if there were the plow would blow them out. Inside my own ears the folds are folding trying to block the power of the volume, and though I can still hear me slightly shouting over the motor, the words I hear are not the words I've said. For instance, I say, "How did I end up riding on a plow here in this smoke cloud in a space of nothing?" and I hear my voice say in reply in the crowding: "Give me everything I want."

I say, "What happened to the person I was after, the person behind me, the persons I knew in all those other days, where did anybody go besides me?" and I hear my dumb self growl in the slush, "The best thing about life in America is my pussy and this pushpin and my balls."

Out of my mouth, see, through the helmet's spigot, also, my mouth is helping with the smoke. Each word I say is part and parcel of the helmet and the air, through which, on the humming plow, which has me glowing, I rumble on the nowhere field.

At certain places in the fold of flowing my vessel bumps into a force: a stream or fat of something hard or otherwise compelling in the flood of spume coming off my ride. I mean the plow will no longer in the run go onward, coming flat and hard against a dais, or the wanting face of someone's homestead, or a mountain, or a machine.

In friction, plow and I, we'll press hard to the pinion of the collision until the object gives in, fumbling over, or I otherwise decide to turn—the toggle levers hard and stumpy between my fingers, covered with little bumps I like to rub. I find sometimes too that I can't take my hand or fingers off the levers even when I want to and the seat sticks to my ass. The rumble in my tummy screams with pudding getting pushed out of my cells, which is better than you'd imagine.

In the smoke I knock a whole lot of big shit down. I lay it out and hear it crackle, squeal or topple, hear its shape diminished, pushed out of the way. The helmet makes me giggle and soaks up all my sound, spit it out as if I'm shrieking ideas at the light.

"THIS IS MY HOUSE," I hear me freaking.

The grinding and rubbing of the plow and machines or buildings or what have you make even more smoke coming out.

The smoke becomes a curtain then it becomes a sash.

The smoke sucks hard all at once into the center of my chest and I am again in my kitchen smashing the plow into the wall.

"THERE IS NO US"

Then I am in the backyard with the workers ripping buried shit up out of the ground. I know Spanish and I am screaming. I eat all the food they have: crystal pancakes, Lifing Wafers, laughter of the bee, bunny pellets, crash dots, Little Sunday, perfect sneeze frame. Each eaten item makes me eat more until the items are my arms.

Then I'm upside down underneath the plow and getting squashed beneath it, the engine's lugs searing my stomach, jutting hard to fit in the small space between my ribs where fat will puddle on the years when I do not stay fit.

Then I am with the men again and all our machines are bashing hard into my house. Bashing hard into the blood stairwell, which is still there, and ends now in a nothing but refracting light, like ice filled up with power and ready to grow old. Most of the blood stairwell has already crumbled, making it impossible to climb, if one wanted, if one could—however, from the ice landing a second stairwell begins, rising up toward another level, an underbelly made of black, blotting out some tiny section of the sun, stunted with light.

I believe there is someone up there. I am always believing.

In the rhythm of our bashing, my house becomes compacted inch by inch. "Motherfuck your fuckhouse!" the workers are screaming, in their language, and, lo, I join in, in mine. "We hate your house! Your house is the house that ruined the other houses all our lives! Your house is the hole of unholy houses filled with holes! We say, again, say, Kill your shithole house, kill it!" I have my hands up over my head. I am so happy, to be destroying, even something so long paid for in my name. Though again, through the helmet, and in the noise, which does not affect them, my language changes to something else, "WHEN WE ARE FINISHED WITH THE DESTRUCTION OF MY PROPERTY WE SHALL DESTROY ME ALSO, TOO! WE WILL RIP ME LIMB FROM LIMB LIKE SOMEONE SHITTY, AS I CERTAINLY WITHOUT QUESTION AM. PLEASE PREPARE INSIDE YOUR MIND FOR THIS INCOMING MISSION, WHICH I WILL NOT DEFEND AGAINST AT ALL."

In the remainder of the time through which we beat the hell out of my house I think about what I just exactly heard me say. I see the eyes of men around me, seeing sideways, their eyes aimed away from and right on into my eyes, their big blue muscles hulked from years of making damage or making progress or feeding selves and wives and child. I see their thoughts about what they will do in return to my invite with their bodies upon mine, thrown hard around inside their head down long veins through their skulls which have been shaved by Corrections three times daily to keep them exposed, in the light.

My plow, compared to their machines, seems older, weakened, grimey. Even my smoke is no beauty like their smoke, rising up into the lid of nowhere like the smallest birds you've ever seen, aimed at the moon.

My helmet squeezes me to listen.

I pay attention to my hands.

I help and help and help out in the fission of our furor as we beat my house apart.

Bang.

We crush the slip of crap that has become spackled to the far side of the kitchen and break the air inside there into the out. I can smell the stink of all my years around me coming from there, spooting out. I had not realized in the center how my kitchen smelled like butt, like someone crying blood into a crown of carrots mixed with baby rash and cud. In fission with the outdoor air the smell blind my eyes a smidge, and I can't see anything but waver where the stink comes pouring out. Balloons.

The men around me vomit also, laughing for my mind. Two men hit the ground and spasm on it, my stink reflexive. We expose a little brine color. Rising at the sky the smell of all my hours makes a small curtain obscuring certainly the rasp of color without size, where the moon has rubbed the sky into contusion, our national obelisk. My blackness clinging to the nothing of the every hour every way. My blackness I've worn underneath my armpits and in my blouse and in my hair, parted where my folds grow, which is why likely there has never been another hand.

I watch until among the height the cloud kisses softly and abrades the nothing as is gone, and again the moon is looking and I am the master of the plow.

Minus the two men, still convulsing, halfway sunken in the earth, me and the men with our machines, we beat the shit out of the kitchen hole. We crush it for its knowing, for what it has let out, what it's made. I am screaming all along me, the hair lining my arms and thighs in braids.

We crush out a ream of parrots. A leaving storm of feathers, shit. Something sinks into the ground inside the light of coming outside in the room where there are stains of someone once having inside become born.

We smash the food closet, with its meat sticks and its pudding powders and its wheat; we smash the cabinets full of bone cloth and the brass bowls stained with the years to get the meat and pudding in; we smash the sinkhole where we poured the extra every evening, feeding something larger than us underneath the house; we smash the light bulbs and the seat assignments and the kitchen table, tall as me. We take turns, in a rhythm, our metal masters heaving in the routine of the maneuver, already becoming old, as though I am sweating and feel pleasure, my center is solid, cold. I want to go to bed. I need nothing. And still I cannot stop my arms. I feel the name of want.

From the crush of what my kitchen was, the crashing leads onto one of three more rooms, each skirting from that center into ventricles of my fine, enormous house, which had not seemed ever quite so large as right now, in its destroy.

In the house now there is a mouth.

Through the mouth I fit me in there, my engine ripped between my legs, the power coursing in the shudder of the pistons and the light.

Down the house's open center, I ride as if in a day parade. From inside, the damage done from out there looks more incidental. The small jut of purple insulation busting from the new pucker where one of us bumped hard with our groan. Roll marks in the hallway where the teeth of someone stuttered in, unlocked a hole beneath the house into which I cannot see more than three feet. Something ever under and overgrown. The house now coming down around it.

I realize I've never touched a lock. Never a crow, a crack, a cookie, never anyone named John. I've never had a fingernail longer than I am. Never took a picture of myself with my eyes closed. I can't stop thinking of what I have not done.

I turn the plow toward the sunroom, where I learned to burn my skin. I roll hard into the blowhole we have ruptured in the house, while the other men go other ways with theirs. In the sunroom, aimed for breaking, centered by windows, I come to stop. The folded chairs of all my sweating and the wrinkles I'd asked in. The little lamp lid you'd use to hide your face with, a ream of mirrors made to shine. The books I think I was supposed to take into me but instead used to shade my sensitives. In the sunroom, suddenly runny, I turn off my machine.

Through the house, under my breathing, I can hear them taking down the walls, the rummage and the pummel of the nights unleashed every seam.

I wait.

I put my hands up to feel the warm glow pulling, but through the glass of windows something is roaring. Something blocked over where the sun pulls, and I can't aim me right, my spine half-crooked in the room temperature sunroom. My spine swishing out from both my sides, like plates of new fat, names of me.

From up high on the plow I am retired, jewels on my fingers tips, a sweater that reads my name. Little divots in my upper lip and on my thorax, which seems to have disappeared. When did I ever have a thorax?

I am laughing. I am all wet. My knees shaking in the power of the house around me getting smaller, as through the walls now the sound is louder and I can hear the wishing of the men, the power coming straight out of their mouths like speech would, though they are thinking and I want to be alone. Through the sun windows, at the center, the other someone standing right there, looking in, wearing a helmet again that obscures their head again and their breathing in my brain.

I want to eat. His or her hands on both side of the glass, both knocking, telling someone other than me to begin. His or hers.

The plow sticks to my belly and my thigh meat and my curves. Its seat and pedals stick to wherever they have touched me and my sweat is not enough. I hear the beating of the machines getting louder. I hear me getting louder inside me, the helmet also around my head and not around my head.

The knocking getting harder. The machines' snarl.

I have a rash.

The plow is sinking in the sunroom's floor, going mushy, into mud. It's the engine that is sparking and is telling jokes into the air.

HOW MANY MOTHERS DOES IT TAKE

TO MAKE A BABY BIGGER THAN ALL NIGHT?

WHAT DO YOU CALL A WHITE HOLE

WITH NO SURNAME AND A THIRST TO INJECT GOD?

I NEED MY MOUTH INSIDE ME

WHERE YOUR MOUTH IS ALWAYS MINE.

The plow beneath me too is seating, skin hole showing where I drip.

Those aren't even jokes you're telling! I scream inside me and it comes out ha ha hahhahahhh ahahahhhahahha hah hah hah aha hha hah ahh aha hahahahahahhahahah ahahhahah ahha ha ha ha ha ha hahahha h a hhh aha hahhhahahha hah h ahhah ahahha hah ahhaha hahahahah ah-hahahah ahahhahah ahhahahahaha ahhah ahahaha hah h ahhahahahha hahahhaha hahahahahahhahahah ahahhahah ahhah a hahaha ha ha-hahha h a hhh aha hahhhahahha hah h ahhah ahahha hah ahhaha hah ah ah ah ahh ah aha h ah ahh a h ah ahh ah ah aha ha hah ah ah ah ahh ah aha h ah ahh a h ah a h h a h a h aha h a hahaha ha hahahha h a hhh aha hahhhahahha hah h ahhah ahahha hah ahhaha hah ah ah ah ahh ah aha h ah ahh a h ah ahh ah ah aha ha hah ah ah ah ahh ah aha h ah ahh a h ah a h h a h a ahhahahahaha hahahahhahahhhahahahhhahahha hah h ahhahahahha hahahhaha hahahahah ah h aha h aa h ah a h h a h a h aha h a hahaha ha hahahha ahhaha hah ah ah ah ahh ah aha h ah ahh a h ah ahh ah ah aha ha hah ah ah ah ahh ah aha h ah ahh a h ah a h h a h a h aha h a hahaha ha hahahha h a hhh aha hahhhahahha hah h ahhah ahahha hah ahhaha hah ah ah ah ha ha hahhahahhh ahahahhhahahha

hah hah hah aha hha hah ahh aha hahahahahahhahahah ahahhahah ahha
ha ha ha ha ha hahahha h a hhh aha hahhhahahha hah h ahhah ahahha
hah ahhaha hahahahah ahhahahah ahahhahah ahhahahahaha ahhah aha-
haha hah h ahhahahahha hahahhaha hahahahahahhahahah ahahhahah
ahhah a hahaha ha hahahha h a hhh aha hahhhahahha hah h ahhah
ahahha hah ahhaha hah ah ah ah ahh ah aha h ah ahh a h ah ahh ah ah
aha ha hah ah ah ah ahh ah aha h ah ahh a h ah a h h a h a h aha h a ha-
haha ha hahahha h a hhh aha hahhhahahha hah h ahhah ahahha hah ah-
haha hah ah ah ah ahh ah aha h ah ahh a h ah ahh ah ah aha ha hah ah
ah ah ahh ah aha h ah ahh a h ah a h h a h a ahhahahahaha hahahahha-
hahhhahahahhhahahha hah h ha ha hahhahahhh ahahahhhahahha hah
hah hah aha hha hah ahh aha hahahahahahhahahah ahahhahah ahha ha
ha ha ha ha hahahha h a hhh aha hahhhahahha hah h ahhah ahahha hah
ahhaha hahahahah ahhahahah ahahhahah ahhahahahaha ahhah ahahaha
hah h ahhahahahha hahahhaha hahahahahahhahahah ahahhahah ahhah
a hahaha ha hahahha h a hhh aha hahhhahahha hah h ahhah ahahha hah
ahhaha hah ah ah ah ahh ah aha h ah ahh a h ah ahh ah ah aha ha hah
ah ah ah ahh ah aha h ah ahh a h ah a h h a h a h aha h a hahaha ha ha-
hahha h a hhh aha hahhhahahha hah h ahhah ahahha hah ahhaha hah
ah ah ah ahh ah aha h ah ahh a h ah ahh ah ah aha ha hah ah ah ah ahh
ah aha h ah ahh a h ah a h h a h a ahhahahahaha hahahahhahahhhaha-
hahhhahahha hah h ha ha hahhahahhh ahahahhhahahha hah hah hah
aha hha hah ahh aha hahahahahahhahahah ahahhahah ahha ha ha ha
ha ha hahahha h a hhh aha hahhhahahha hah h ahhah ahahha hah ah-
haha hahahahah ahhahahah ahahhahah ahhahahahaha ahhah ahahaha
hah h ahhahahahha hahahhaha hahahahahahhahahah ahahhahah ahhah
a hahaha ha hahahha h a hhh aha hahhhahahha hah h ahhah ahahha hah
ahhaha hah ah ah ah ahh ah aha h ah ahh a h ah ahh ah ah aha ha hah
ah ah ah ahh ah aha h ah ahh a h ah a h h a h a h aha h a hahaha ha ha-
hahha h a hhh aha hahhhahahha hah h ahhah ahahha hah ahhaha hah
ah ah ah ahh ah aha h ah ahh a h ah ahh ah ah aha ha hah ah ah ah ahh
ah aha h ah ahh a h ah a h h a h a ahhahahahaha hahahahhahahhhaha-
hahhhahahha hah h ha ha hahhahahhh ahahahhhahahha hah hah hah
aha hha hah ahh aha hahahahahahhahahah ahahhahah ahha ha ha ha
ha ha hahahha h a hhh aha hahhhahahha hah h ahhah ahahha hah ah-
haha hahahahah ahhahahah ahahhahah ahhahahahaha ahhah ahahaha

hah h ahhahahahha hahahhaha hahahahahahhahahah ahahhahah ahhah a hahaha ha hahahha h a hhh aha hahhhahahha hah h ahhah ahahha hah ahhaha hah ah ah ah ahh ah aha h ah ahh a h ah ahh ah ah aha ha hah ah ah ah ahh ah aha h ah ahh a h ah a h h a h a h aha h a hahaha ha hahha h a hhh aha hahhhahahha hah h ahhah ahahha hah ahhaha hah ah ah ah ahh ah aha h ah ahh a h ah ahh ah ah aha ha hah ah ah ah ahh ah aha h ah ahh a h ah a h h a h a ahhahahahaha hahahahhahahhhaha-hahhhahahha hah h ahh ah h a hhh aha hahhhahahha hah h ahhah ahahha hah ahhaha hah ah ah ah ahh ah aha h ah ahh a h ah ahh ah ah aha ha hah ah ah ah ahh ah aha h ah ahh a h ah a h h a h a h aha h a.

On my chest the spit is winning, making holes in me too, like the home.

Through the glass the other who is laughing also but it comes out in all words: I tried to tell you doing the same. It was doing the same every day. There was doing the same every motion you could make. You kept doing the same things and the days kept frying and you knew to understand. You knew every inch of what was missing doing the same or what you had right there doing the same and you kept walking room to room doing the same with your whole mouth full and the terror in your mind doing the same. This is your way. This is money. Every inch of ours doing the same.

The plow now halfway lodged down in the sun mud, slicking down with both big wheels, grinding gushed into the magma of the new floor, drawing a tunnel, stunted, roared—as where I can feel the earth beneath me wants us under the plow itself cannot make sense, is rolling hard and coughing in the goo wet, up to my ankles in what a mess.

My blood starts coming out my nose again and trickling along my back, where in its streaming I can hear singing or at least someone wishing me along.

Through the walls, becoming nearer, I hear the men destroy my bedroom and my den. I hear them rip the books up, eat the mattress, smash the crap out of my dresser, what I am. I hear the flat tines of the machines' teeth crush through the wall that keeps the foyer from the night, and through the husk of cells that hold the bathroom and the hallway apart, the flesh of my whole house. At five sides they worm around me unmaking while I pour.

I want to help. My other me or her whoever beats the windows with two fists. With four fists, then whole heads. The helmet chinks against the glass. The glass splays into partitions but no bending, a pattern of the vein. I see my name writ in the break, and in seeing it becomes no longer mine.

[•]

A history.

Shaped like a flounder.

Smelling of *une autre semaine.*

Spoken in French, or in France. *Ici,* on *parle à la fin du mois.* On *parle de cela en fin de semaine.* On *aime les marguerites.* On *n'aime pas les marguerites. Ce n'est guère raisonnable. C'est comme des meubles.*

The gist of it is that if one wants to see something, say something. Exclamation mark. Comma. Dash. Comma. Semicolon. Inverted comma. Dash. Comma. Comma. Comma. Semicolon. Comma. Comma. Comma. Comma. Comma inverted comma. Comma. Colon. Comma. Dash. Comma. Inverted comma. Comma. Period. Number seven. Exclamation mark. Inverted comma. Comma. Period. Comma. Comma. Comma. Semicolon. Inverted comma. Inverted comma. Inverted comma. Period. Period. Comma. Comma. Exclamation mark. Question mark. Comma. Comma. Comma. Dash. Colon. Comma. Comma. Period. Number ten. Say something. Say it again.

The interest that one takes in the present is always contingent upon its being present, a radical enough act of contingency itself. One therefore can ask too much of the present by way of demanding a constant fidelity to this kind of history, that is, history in the making. In order to prove one's true interest in the present, one must be willing for it to be absolutely situated in the past, in other words, to be history as one knows and loves history, that present which has already been decided upon.

Walls. White.

Looking.

Looking.

For the person in the white. Looking for black skin in a white head, by any body's given name.

Bracton (circa 1250) seemed to be fairly complacent with the jury as an institution. Other contemporaneous writers were markedly dissatisfied with the jury. This is how one will hereafter refer to the way that one will see things or will have said to have seen them. One believes this will make one an expert in this regard. The 'Mirror of Justice' contains a violent attack on the jury system from 1290. It is not uncommon for someone like oneself to be somewhat misunderstood in the early reception and then later misunderstood completely. Thus allowing for future success. Marginalia, in a word. One wonders if there will be a dinner later. One would like some speeches, followed by the clanging of plates, upper and lower. An other might wish for something else to be said. Once one prayed for a vision. One told the other this, and the other told one that one had a view and not to be so particular. The other was right, of course. Situationally. How one lives in piece. One never got one's name. Someone wrote that the criterion for deciding whether a city was modern was the absence of monuments. One never got the name, though one agreed to despise the countryside, squatting there in abashed unamazement. Singing the Ding. The ich-dich. There is always fourteen.

I have a lamp around my own skull, new duds. I can't see beyond the small part where my hair curls down around me. It is not my hair. Grown from the ass of the sky and flying in the wind of nothing gone. No one is gone. The white is black, too.

Looking for the person in the black. Black skin in a black year.

I want me all over again.

I feel my fingers up my rectum and pull them out and see they are not mine. The presence up my gut still sits hard, coagulated, as I sniff my fingers for the night. Both my middle fingers have been stitched up hard with blue lace.

I poke around on what's filled in my low hole. It's hardened hard, a concrete brittle prism, a blockade blocking off.

Too, I see, my mouth: it has a lid set in it. I cannot taste anything at all. Foam. And my nostrils and my ear holes. I am stuffed up. Through my eyes I feel my eyes.

Walls. Now several colors, flood-rotating through a groan where with each thought the walls do new hues—gold, gold, gold, pink, gold, ash, chalk—so on—in my belly there is the singlemost sensation of the thickness spreading, coloring me in. Filling my centermost hole also.

What can I do outside me without eyes, without teeth that cut or breathing? How am I breathing, stuck, and why?

I don't need answers to keep eating where I feel my tummy eating me alive.

In the off balance I feel me reel. I am standing wholly up. I am unmoored to any even where the walls are. I can move through all. All of what the nothing is surrounding. I can laugh a lot inside, though what the laugh does is make putty of the ground beneath me and I fall. I fall and I am falling. The walls not in color, but of sound. Saying in collision.

My blood is made of hair. My hair is made of a stretch of land in West Virginia that I know soon will be sold. On the land someone will build a reservation. The reservation will be burned. A casino will be built on the ashes in their scrunched glisten. The light will go for years. One of my 15,000 children will enter the casino through the smallest door on an evening in which all birds have become calm. He will bet the farm on black, then leave the table without waiting. He will purchase room 3114. He will go into room 3114 and leave the key on the floor outside the doorway. He will lie down on the bed.

I buy and sell a house in West Virginia in my mind. Thereafter the house is nowhere and the sun is cunning light: a ball like the two balls sets in the scrotum of the son I will not have. I can feel my fifty thousand sons wriggle inside me while the plow goes putty with the sea once made of dirt. The earth crumbling beneath me but not letting me in, like more machines down there I had not hired or been party to at all.

I feel this in my present action, written on my knuckles in blue print. I bring a fist to dap the whoever I can in the air before me and hit nothing and become slightly bigger boned.

My hair is made of the goldest things and this room is not small at all.

I don't need to talk about the walls because when I say whatever about them they always move against whatever I have said, as where now inside the white of my holes plugged in the destruction in the sunroom's flutter up my butt, I see the light some have named god. I raise my arm to rub my fingers through god's gone gold mane of no glisten and

and
and
and

I am, in my holes, inverted

where my holes were, filled, before me, the meat around those holes now is all gone

burnt like someone's stupid money and less than me I am now me

I am walking so hard and fast inside the white hill I can see me there again before me waiting, my shoulders nothing, my speech a bone. My me in this instance resembles someone who's been abandoned in a fire, like the fire of the gravel in my butt, rumping, lipping, pilling up my middle with its seize. I don't have time for this, I mention aloud to anybody, and I don't know what I mean. I've never not had time for every hour and this one is not extant, and I am still right here inside me and above me and behind, though each step of me comes on in perfect rhythm, and so

I'd never know, except: I know. And in our each step, too, the sound of machines still ever in me, making mulch of what I am, my wish, these years.

In the cold of no clear color I smush on, rolling, my ab muscles saying why. My neck a triple double roll of paper products used some year to clean the mess out of the sheets. The long bed of unmade people gifting glue into the light, which in warbling from my ex-center spills out beneath me in a sodden, gray-green plume. I clench my hand to feel it and in my hand I have the long knife.

I have the knife that's made of bread sperm. Bread of sperm I had inside me from the spurting or the make. Bread from what I wanted and could not have. Bread of terrifying bright.

I fold the bread into the machine gun I always wanted in my life. The gun is empty. I hear mice. I hear someone right beside me also hefting, limb by limb, so on. Ahead I see me running from me and I am not the same one of me at all.

I blow my breath into the nozzle and load it with the zip, with the incantation of my belly and the backwards words I've let sit wedged in my gums for decades. The rot of flue makes me feel lumpy. The gun is heavy. I am wet.

I take fire. Then I aim.

My bullets spray the season with the well that I've kept tapped in the pocket about my liver, blackening by day and day; in the pustules on my aorta that in certain lights here make my chest seem caving; and in the lighter strands of my eyelashes fluttered fine. My bullets of my worst choices sent to rattle at the sky of nothing and the arc of nothing underneath called the earth, and at the nothing of something that is all between each inch of us around here, this city too in its relief.

Up my arms, holding the machine gun, I watch the pill-shaped varmints scatter out, coursing up my limbs in twin directions on the outlines of my veins to trundle down my fingers to the trigger and the body of the gun itself—the gun I already have finished with, in shooting, before me now peering through the glassy curl to see magnified what I can see, though here the mist of my breath obscures the lenslook so quickly, and what with the dotted lines meant to help me hit right, I can hardly make out any place or target mark at all.

Still, along the long arm of it, made of my bread, in my arms, I can see not only me there far ahead still running, not shot, but the farther me ahead of that, and there, ahead of that one, another me there also running, the hair grown longer, legs less arched. For each further me that I can count out of the white of nothing way on out there, in the stream of cream and pee, I'm that much smaller, that much closer to a knob or button to be pressed upon the face of nothing to produce an effect I may or may not judge. A bump mark to be bumped on. All of my heads at different turning angles. All my arms splayed into crooks and lather, a mess of limbs none of we can count. Some of me here and there inside the fortune will look back with certain steps to see who is here of me behind them and yet none of them seem to see any of the others of me here inside here.

Set up in my aim again I shoot. I pop to fire off another auction of my liquid and my come, my ideas in the fission, assassinate me in the back. I aim to fire and sing sweetly in the trigger with me, my mouth all crumby and excited with the knock off of this not quite next of kin.

BANG, I scream, quoting, then pull the trigger, grunting, shitting in my pants.

BANG, I go, and feel me in me sizzle. So so good.

None of me at all will fall. All of me up there keep on running undistracted. Through the aiming lens I see them still ongoing as even in the wet of me I stop. Some misfire. My eggs are bumping in my stomach at my lungs.

I want.

I go to blow more bullets of me into the gun's mouth with my wetness, but my lips no longer fit around the bit. The muzzle having swollen so large it is my arm completely, it is my chest completely, it is me. I want.

I am in the gun.

I am, me, surrounded, by the blackest light I've ever seen. The blacklight pounding my lungs and areolas, in my tongue and in my teeth. I reach up in my cheeks to try to see enough to have a chew to gnaw through the pulp of metallic unglow packing my cerebrum, but I cannot make my meat part. My meat of no old holes, set up in the resin of my making, and my spreading stutter. I try to turn in the long column and it sticks to me, skin on skin, wholly numbered, until inside the gun the light in sudden gust lights striking, filling any inch where I am old, filling every path of jump around me, and I gush.

LET ME OUT OF ME

I hear me screaming, not what I meant to say at all—the jury system—and in the crust of night I hear my inverse creaking, spilling into down—English courts—the gluebells ringing in my innards—OUCH OUCH OUCH OUCH OUCH—the public at large, reluctance to accept juries on a large scale—the pump of bubbles booing whole crowds off my body, sloughing in the speech— the outcome of a duel, or from some ordeal—my speech of any instant, saying nothing, black gifts in the soft ball of my spit—a sporadic appearance in England—Danelaw and the Saxons—saliva raining on the nothing in the evening of the hour of the night—even so, even so, juries had never been predominant—prominent. Say it again. Prevalent. Say it again. Prominent. Say it again. Say it again. Say it.

I Utterance Two

We are two of us, both one;
bigger than a Screaming Machine, smaller than a hole.

OR:

Exit strategy.

[○]

One of those spindly, hollow-eyed countrysides, soft at the edges, which jiggled when it walked, and sloped unattractively over the tops of its pants, its wrists too thin, and its skies painted, they seemed painted, with dull menace, like a tin-roofed shed. Precisely. Geometrically, if one can be so abstract. In the hard sweat of the first of many cities I come down in slow droves. Thick, mean. One understands completely. That is the great and ongoing concern. A real business, to which one bicycles from every day, pockets, if one had pockets, stuffed with receipts and the stubs of yellow pencils. One understands tenements, comprehends ghettos. The better neighborhoods are nothing to one. In those parts of France where the jury system took root at the same time, there were tremendous protests against it, as being oppressive. So many stanzas seeking a chorus of old hens. One wishes one had time to say everything, now that one is alone. One thing one would note, if one had a stub of yellow pencil, is the decline in birthrates. There is no similar decline in interest. Originally due to economic straits, dire, it had, by this time, become appealingly general. It should be noted that the fact—a lovely thing, quite dependent on a certain amount of disquiet and theatricality—that ordinary people, by which one means highly cultivated, consider the question of reproduction a matter of cost and benefits, pro's and con's, this ways and that ways, a matter of tips and advice and low-cost alternatives to going out or the lives of objects. From the time of Edward I of England onward, the function of the jury was slowly being judicially defined. Would like to point out how faithfully one has adhered to the law of mustn't say. Still. Like that. Silence is a virtue. There's some. Say again. Did one forget? There's some again. Questions of law were being separated from questions of fact. Just missed that one. It's called tentative architecture.

In the hard sweat of the first of many cities I come down in slow droves. The cycle of enforced weather over our remaining bodies mandates no more than an arm's length in one burst, and so the condensation of my lungs and lids and small intestine for some hours clog the sun. A pattern rashed on the field gridlock, killing corn and wheat to stay unfed, made sodden into mazes in which kids will get lost and go missing and become skinmaps composed to sink in earthy chub. They go on being begotten in the anus of the spirit of the life of our soft god, from the tongue of where I've lived in walking, waking, for the centuries of my half-life. The white scraped slather on my tongue this morning, glossy, where from the city in the sky I am.

For the cities in their prisms underneath me I pour worms. Through blue openings on both sides of my forehead the flue is gluey and makes me want to eat, to refill the gap of magic with Corn Flakes and breadcrumbs, party wieners and fried rice. I don't have any money and no shirt on. Gas stations on the cities' sacs glow clean, in slim distraction for the caving of the earth and my oncoming, of which I am not the only one. My others in the sky beside me, trying, spittled downward upside down. From up here I can read the language of the hole my house has made upon the system of the candy of the night, caved in to spit back at me with the breath of mantle and of core.

But I am coming down. This earth, anyway, a soft one in the light of where I've been before. Every hour counting down becoming cleaner, neater pinned, cut in the collar of my shirt, to choke and chafe and maybe one day be a dressing gown for someone's child, in the recycle of our garments so the recycle of our skin. Flesh and sperm and money and the pistons of a car. The black bear in any being. Funny oceans. Overworked and underpaid. Or something.

Oh yes I am coming down—down upon me from the motion at the center of the eye, cut into the fabric of the nothing where the babies come and drink, come to sit inside some fold of snowing that I get old within my sneering face shape. I mean that here in the drip of my destruction I am poured again into the night, wet with liquor exhale and bone smoking and the rattle of the drumtraps, as in the meat below me of the second self the men have given over working for the stomp and furor of the beat of it, collected in reflective surfaces for flexing to pound the fists and stomp the stump. Men with big eyes and mind erasers going spastic on boxes, boards, the surfaces of buildings and of air itself. Blood percussion of the nothing-left-to-eat.

I pour through me, of my center, and am again set into this earth. Again into the index of bees and future children and the want I cannot hide on the skins of all the thrumming men I glisten for a minute, mixed with sweat that stinks. I slick into their hair and hum their skin. I spread in darkness through the pockets of their pants and down their legs and knuckles and leak in silence to the ground. The pummel of the drums contorts my surface, blurting the sky back itself. The sky of my forehead has six eyes in it. The eyes of me and me and mine, and who is that. I am watching me watch me watch me watch.

In the soil my body mixes: gold and coffee, gravel, ice; tree worms and the worms I've just let out from my intestines, already blooming skyward in the bright mask the night deforms: their husks becoming tents over the new door of the new day in this air. Canopies and t-shirts in the windows of an air that cannot breathe. Overhead, while in my pooling, I can smell the night becoming wet, and the wet becoming night again. And hours turning slaw. The drums so loud in echoed beef I cannot hear them but their reflection, the shudder of our atmospheres and apertures in skin.

From the mud I come culled, stand up. The hall of my three fists.

Bugs are crawling up my pretend womb spot, getting it pregnant, flying out of my bellybutton to go somewhere underneath me even further inside the soil and make more like them.

Apples in my teeth and writing, biting themselves biting themselves.

I open my new mouth and butter comes out: chocolate, sunshine, pepper, and cornsilk. I inhale and taste my acid, passed down ages in what a brain is.

I am happy as a pilgrim. Overworked and underpaid. Or something.

My pretend testicles are rock, shook from the face of what was once an altar or a grocery store or wedding rings.

Overhead I hear the wall. I hear the me that let me fizzle saying words I have already madly said in repetition, in going on.

There is not a language I can speak now, but by making bumps inside my head all spilling crap like frightened pigeons in the biscuits of our mud underneath us. I am right down here.

Now the fright is spitting up.

Now the crack of guns I became in me come back washing and lick all up the center of my guts giving shape by wet of being and tongue definition so I can hurl. Throw both my hard arms towards the over-forehead, which Corrections has already appended with new screaming bulbs, the colors of my thoughts enplasmed with them, hulking as an infant at a thrall.

In the blank of drums in my new standing I hear a shrieking and with my nose I turn around inside the smell of these years already pressed upon us stitching up my nostrils and pinching in crafty lines of neon ants. My head's weight rotates on an axis that descends into my tummy, tucked with the nothing in kaput. No more blood and no more cellmake, no more doors or potions.

Behind me stand the women with the hands shaped like my hands. In their hands, though, are microphones, with wires strung straight upwards to the glowing, a rubber charcoal-colored Christmas tree. Women without number, shoulder to shoulder, shore to shore, cut by a line. On this side, them; on that side, me. We mirrored, X to 1.

The women open up their mouths together. I feel mine open too.

The women with the hair down to their asses grown in soft with the bush over their buttocks and their grout. Hair growing longer. Hair down the throat stopping the singing, stopping the round.

In my hand no mic, but a blue globe. A ball big as my center heart is—that is, not large. This one is ribbed. Sticky and immensely perforated, so much that it looks smooth. A little raw spot in its top lip bears an inscription I cannot read.

Our mouths continue all done open while I hold the organ out over my head. The microphones conducting nothing from the choir of our snug flesh. The silent snap of our paused breathing awaiting.

Behind me, a tower rises from beneath. A protein tower throttling the sky. I feel its heat as it erupts and rises through the center of the scrawl and signage overhead and parts the light. Around the tower, from the long soil, rise too many smaller towers, in the image. One for each of us compelled.

The dividing line between my sight and there behind me is the color of the pig. I do not try to turn to see the towers. I look into these women's eyes. In the prisms of their unsweating I can see the mechanisms of their belief systems and want for eating. The towers yet to make a sound.

Unto our mouths in blackened palates, cruddy gums. The microphones and their long wires, plugged in unblinking to continue shushed and sing the zip out of our lives. The hair a necklace worn in summers. Hair a curtain, window, outfit, and something to rub against deformed. My coffee snoring in me perfect. White light in buckets turned upward in the endless braying brink of overhead and there beyond where.

In our slay of praise.

In the disease of no condition, yours and whose.

Drums with water on their top skins so the wet skitters back into the drummers' face parts. My face and faces parted. My gold wet. I wait. I inhale me. I, again: unbone.

I reach toward the gog of the this ungoing pleasure, all arms, my skin pitching tiny tents and wrists arrayed in white wedding rings made too wide.

I force my whole organ in my small mouth. I bite down in its resin, squirting sand dry. The bubble of gross oil fills my soft place in disposed orchestra. The heartmeat knees my teeth out, wraps my bonnet, clogs me pink. I can no longer see the women, though in the rasp I hear them caw. The sound as loud lunged as the drums were, the drums here having too returned, voices in a ash-paste frenzy clustered around my head, filling the air, then the air red, then the air my liver's shade, parsing each bark of blonde and brunette, grayed out and dark as night locked through my guts.

I chew my vessels like a hamburger, while behind my back the towers clang. The many tiny towers leaning in my shadow to touch the center-most rung, the central prong, thickening in light and neon to be all of them at once and so again.

And in the soup of us I'm choking not to breathe, but to be choked.

And in the collision of the sung seconds and the wires, I become turned around—turned again to stand beneath the pill-shaped tower, the tower bell-shaped radiating and unstenched, Its open mouth, too, talking, leaning over, coming down. Into my open mouth, my best remaindered hole. My gross, negated eye. Raincoats, mean. As if there were such a thing. But one becomes disorganized. What one wants to see is a vision. Arguments centered around questions like: Is a jury conclusion of 11 to 1 enough to convict for a crime? This one has noted in pencil. It is part of one's doing one's part to increase stress in the workplace. As if. As if nothing could be said. Dread and apprehension, that's what's had. In place of. In place of a real job. In place. Dangerous witness. One or the other. Though this is the secret, the real time-saver. As if. No job. Just dread and apprehension. This allows one to spend one's time much more efficiently, going straight to the heart of the matter, of the job, that is, any job, without the collateral time spent on doing the something something to provoke the same effect. Affect, mean. As if. Later this week new figures will be released which will reveal the extent of the relationship between event and stress and then revise accordingly. There will be refreshments, and some singing. In 1468, Sir John Fortescue gives a picture of jury trials which is congruent with the modern form. A memo will be circulated to this effect among upper management.

Childless. Architectureless. Overworked and underpaid. Or something.

One wishes one had a desk to lay one's head upon. The jury had come to be regarded as twelve men who could be of open mind. One wishes one had a briefcase. As if. Later one will attempt to reduce the case one has, turn it into a mere pleading, or better still, a doe-eyed look. A sense of justice. Cool and refreshing. Cast over the moors, or the man at the sink who bears an uncanny resemblance to the neighbor one had as a child. Witnesses were examined under oath. It was a worldwide movement, something we would remember forever.

[○]

The center spiral of the tower is the same width as my spine. One has in mind *a*. The stairs the same color as my monthlies packed into a lid. One has in mind *a*. Each step's height matches as much as I can lift a leg in one move tugging my muscles for the want. I get to work. One has in mind *a*. Today is today.

One has in mind *a*. One has in mind *a*. One has in mind *a*. One has in mind *a*. One has in mind *a*. One has in mind *a*. One has in mind *a*. One has in mind a momentary lapse of viewpoint, a point of view, more precisely. Some things can never be said, proving themselves absolutely.

My anger makes me burp it. Each step I'm up I pump a gift out, new balloons popped between my cheeks and kissing in reverse a flood of putty out onto the stairwell or my hands.

Never alone. Never again. More to the point, one looks forward to it. That is to say, one has no choice.

I cough up a combination lock. I try every combination I can think of but the barbs stay on my thumbs, and the click of the lock between the metal and where the thing spins starts gushing up a bunch of little bells. They stick to me like chiggers. I swallow the lock back and wait to shit.

As an American, one is free to travel wherever one wants. One is free to choose however one wants. One means whoever. One means in the absence of. One means one has no choice but to be wherever one wants. One means to be an American. More wanting. More to be discovered, unsaid.

I am walking up the stairs in silence. For once at last a little I hear no one before or after, or within.

I cough up a pastry shaped from ash. I take the ash against my belly and rub it hard and gather where it gathers and make a gummy roll out of itself. It smells delicious, like the Shop Mart. I want to shove it up a rut. I pull my shorts up and off a little and there is still not any spot.

"Hold still," I say to the special part of me, or where that was sometime and something other.

Remember this: A century later, Sir Thomas Smith gives a vivid account of the jury trial with examination, cross-examination, all in front of the judge and jury. This is another feeling about history, another point of view, pointless. One wishes one had a gun. One wishes one was another one. One wishes one could sing. Or believe. Or be somewhere other than in between.

I am walking up the air. Not quite silence but a rubber still, the kind you can put against you in a bed that has no second body in and spend the whole night right beside the crack of what most everyone calls sleep.

My legs are doing runny. The stairs do little curves.

I cough up, AHAHHHHAHHAAHAHHAHA HAHAH HA HAHAH
HA H HAHHAHAH AHAHHA HA HHA H AHHA AHHA A AHAH-
HHHAHHAAHAHHAHA HAHAH HA HAHAH HA H HAHHAHAH
AHAHHA HA HHA H AHHA AHHA AHAHAAH AA AHAHHH-
HAHHAAHAHHAHA HAHAH HA HAHAH HA H HAHHAHAH
AHAHHA HA HHA H AHHA AHHA A AHAHHHHAHHAAHAH-
HAHA HAHAH HA HAHAH HA H HAHHAHAH AHAHHA HA
HHA H AHHA AHHA A AHAHHHHAHHAAHAHHAHA HAHAH
HA HAHAH HA H HAHHAHAH AHAHHA HA HHA H AHHA
AHHA A AHAHHHHAHHAAHAH H HAHH AHAH AHAHHAHA
HHA H AHHA AHHA A HAHA HAHAH HA HAHAH HA H HAH-
HAHAH AHA HHA HA HHA H AHHA AHHA A AHAHHHHAH-
HAAHAHHAHA HAHAH HA HAHAH HA H HAHHAHAH
AHAHHA HA HHA H AHHA AHHA A AHAHHHHAHHAAHAH-
HAHA HAHAH HA HAHAH HA H HAHHAHAH AHAHHA HA
HHA H AHHA AHHA A H HAHHAHAH AHAHHA HA HHA H
AHHA AHHA A H HAHHAHAH AHAHHA HA HHA H AHHA

AHHA AHAHHA HA HHA H AHHA AHHA A AHAHHHHAHHAA-
HAHHAHA HAHAH HA HAHAH HA H HAHHAHAH AHAHHA
HA HHA H AHHA AHHA A AHAHHHHAHHAAHAH H HAHH
AHAH AHAHHAHA HHA H AHHA AHHA A HAHA HAHAH HA
HAHAH HA H HAHHAHAH AHA HHA HA HHA H AHHA AHHA
A AHAHHHHAHHAAHAHHAHA HAHAH HA HAHAH AHAHHA
HA HHA H AHHA AHHA A H HAHH AHAH A AHAHHAHA
AHAHHHHAHHAAHAHHAHA HAHAH HA HAHAH HA H HAH-
HAHAH AHAHHA HA HHA H AHHA AHHA A AHAHHHHAH-
HAAHAH H HAHH AHAH AHAHHAHA HHA H AHHA AHHA A
HAHA HAHAH HA HAHAH HA H HAHHAHAH AHA HHA HA
HHA H AHHA AHHA A AHAHHHHAHHAAHAHHAHA HAHAH
HA HAHAH A AHAHHHHAHHAAHAHHAHA HAHAH HA
HAHAH HA H HAHHAHAH AHAHHA HA HHA H AHAHHHHAH-
HAAHAHHAHA HAHAH HA HAHAH HA H HAHHAHAH
AHAHHA HA HHA H HHA H AHHA AHHA A AHAHHHHAHHAA-
HAH H HAHH AHAH AHAHHAHA HHA H AHHA AHHA A HAHA
HAHAH HA HAHAH HA H HAHHAHAH AHA HHA A HHA H
AHHA AHHA A AHAHHHAHHAAHAHHAHA HAHAH HA
HAHAH AHAHHA HA HHA H AHHA AHHA A H HAHH AHAH A
AHAHHAHA AHAHHHHAHAAHAHHAHA HAHAH HA HAHAH
HA H HAHHAHAH AHAHHA HA HHA H AHHA AHHA A AHAH-
HHHAHHAAHAH H HAHH AHAH AHAHHAHA HHA H AHHA
AHHA A HHA H AHHA AHHA A AHAHHHHAHHAAHAH H
HAHH AHAH AHAHAHA HHA H AHHA AHHA A HAHA HAHAH
HA HAHAH HA H HAHHAHAH AHA HHA HA HHA H AHHA
AHHA A AHAHHHHAHHAAHAHHAHA HAHAH HA HAHAH
AHAHA HA AHHA A AHAHHHHAHHAAHAHHAHA HAHAH HA
HAHAH A AHAHHHHAHHAAHAHHAHA HAHAH HA HAHAH
HA H HAHHAHAH AHAHHA HA HHA H AHAHH AHHA A
AHAHHHHAHHAAHAHHAHA HAHAH HA HAHAH A AHAHH-
HHAHHAAHAHHAHA HAHAH HA HAHAH HA H HAHHAHAH
AHAHHA HA HHA H AHAHHHHAHHAAHAHHAHA HAHAH HA
HAHAH HA H HAHHAHAH AHAHHA HA HHA H HHA H AHHA
AHHA A AHAHHHHAHHAAHAH H HAHH AHAH AHAHHAHA
HHA H AHHA AHHA A HAHA HAHAH HA HAHAH HA H HAH-

HAHAH AHA HHA A HHA H AHHA AHHA A HHAHHAAHAHHAHA HAHAH HA HAHAH HA H HAHHAHAH AHAHHA HA HHA H HHA H AHHA AHHA A AHAHHHHAHHAAHAH H HAHH AHAH AHAHHAHA HHA H AHHA AHHA A HAHA HAHAH HA HAHAH HA H HAHHAHAH AHA HHA A HHA H AHHA AHHA A HHA H AHHA AHHA A H HAHH AHAH A AHAHHAHA AHAHHHAHHAAHAHHAHA HAHAH HA HAAH HA H HAHHAHAH AHAHHA HA HHA H AHHA AHHA A AHAHHHHAHHAAHAH H HAHH AHAH AHAHHAHA HHA H AHHA AHHA A, again quoting.

Mother hell that is a load of laughing, I tell it, where it withers on the air. It's not even candy. It's a patience I never needed in my life. The tumor of my horny mentalism. Would this lead to a rhetorical gesture. To something something. To the mustn't-say. Most probably, as it implies a certain sense of discovery, as is suggested by any plain, or to put it geometrically, plane. But it is too soon to find anything out. One wonders what time it is. One wonders where it is. Whoever, that is to say. One no longer wonders what. It is not this place. Not yet. There's so much not to say. No matter. Never matter.

I pass a window in the tower without seeing anything through it there at all—though the color of the light is like someone has put a pink blanket over my birdcage and is still standing there outside it blowing breathing in and god it reeks. I see a tumor on my wrist in the shape of a buried watch. I nudge it with my knuckle, hear another grinding of the vice.

"Goddamn my legs are like the Bowflex, and yet I've got the passion in me to do acid blind. In the spit I've had for no one." That's what I say I say I said.

Shortly after the institution of the jury system, with its attendant seeking of evidence, based on testimony given by witnesses, the problem of maintenance developed. Maintenance was the practice of witnesses coming forward to provide testimony at trial, without being asked to do so. They say that dreams define a generation, or one read it somewhere, more likely the latter. One read somewhere that Proust had to have the dreams he had in order to dream up something better than boredom. One read that every generation has its dreams based on its education or religion or distraction, whatever is predominant, available. Proust was disembodied, it can be read. Soutine a bit soft round the edges. Corporeal, meaning. Or was that Saussure. One gets them confused, having no real experience with either of them. These were frequently well meaning friends or family members who wanted to participate, or help sway the verdict of the trial. To be kept apart from their dreams. Kept in an Italian leather-bound journal tied shut with a leather cord. Or rather a leather Italian-bound journal cord in leather. Though one must admit or confess, the latter being a fuller gesture, more complete, as if with jam, that one doesn't dream. Never. Hardly ever. Lack of dominance, one imagines. One doesn't imagine. Hardly ever. Never.

I cough up a plate of biscuits and gum gravy and it looks good enough to eat forever. I leave it on the step for whoever else assuring it will be there when I come back down.

"Yes I will come back down again," I say and say and say and say and then there is a flat level stair as long as god's eye or the sum spread of all our mayonnaise incensed.

A few more steps up I stop hard and spin back and run unto the biscuits I coughed up and scarf them down. Their static grain inside me helps me bleed more and I am smiling with my teeth all old. I am full. In my belly's boom, my false infant mocks my gestures and the ideas I once had.

The flat of stairs again goes so much in such directions and the honey of it is I am four years old. I run as hard and fast in one direction as I can manage with the wind whipping my tonsils. When I reach the far end of my composure there is a blue horse and no matter what I touch about it, it will not move. Its long horse cock plugs into the floor beneath it with a landscape of blue gold qualities. Looking closer, the cock has people on it who scream and jump at me, near to my nose. I turn and run right back where I came from and I am laughing. I am the laughing. Then I am on the stairs again and I am forty and I have purple snow all in my teeth. The Statute of Westminster I (1275) had fifty-one chapters. Any one of which might be in German. Es dürfte auf Deutsch sein. Wie zu erwarten wäre. Das dürfte der Fall sein. Man darf dabei nicht vergessen, dass Zusammenfassend kann man daher sagen, dass Fairnesshalber muss man sagen, dass Anders ist es nicht zu erklären. One of these surely dealt with the issue of maintenance. Or maybe not. What one does find, and this one can say like a real native, that l'histoire fait un pied de moi nez. Put another way, one has found that one's illusions, which have been knowingly substituted for dreams, and for that matter, hopes, though not, one would note, again, if one had the graphite, fantasies, for one's got to have something to hang on to, if there's a free hand in the matter, and one's illusions have the orchestrate feel of compositions, complete with the tap-tap-tap prior to their full execution, and the stray cough of disinterest larded within. One would like to think, and will someday, tomorrow or Tuesday, one has got nothing on Tuesday, though it's got plenty on one or the another, being a constant site of suffering. I cough up teeth. I cough up hair gel. I cough up a length of burning rope. I try to hang myself on a barhook from the stairs' curve but the rope will not stay tied and my neck feels too fat to fit the rope around it and I am walking up and on again.

Ash in patterns on my midsection. My eyes fall out of my head. I cough up new eyes and plug them back in and now the stairs are half sized and purpled with my vein beep, which some others call a pulse.

I pass the conduit of something, the conduit where the stairs from the early portions of this page had appeared, seeming jutted out of nothing but a grapple in slow dark. I have tried all throughout since then to find someone in the white dark and have heard or have not heard, last night, but what is cut into my skin, last night, now is there forever and that is what is done.

Last night, up this little stair I see everything I've done dreamt of.

Dreamt of lapping a lady last night, not a stranger to one, was what you might call a friend, what one might call a friend, in other words, though at some point she removed herself altogether while remaining in the bed, and squatted quite attractively, all right, sexily, at the head of the bed while she enjoyed herself there beneath one's mouth. One gets so very hungry. And all the while one has that strange feeling of being watched, that stranger feeling of being enjoyed. A common enough feeling, that is to say, strange just in its bare familiarity. Being a dream.

I try to say something also aloud about what my first child would have liked to eat or listen to or want or do a touch with but instead I cough up a plastic braid blockade. I place the blockade over where the old steps go so I won't try to look at them again. On the far side of it, in the instant, there forms a flood of flies, gushed like microwaved ice cream. They shout my insides at me, gurgled. They say a sermon's word. The stairs repeat.

I pop a squat on the tower and hear my pee go down in sentences I did not need, which are all of them, every one.

I pass a sign for the Tower Library and cough up chests. Each nipple busts with milk and voices, "she enjoyed herself there beneath one's mouth," echoed through the wires tied into the mammalian cells. My voice is one of those. She enjoyed herself there beneath one's mouth. I am saying nothing new. Nothing new. Nothing new. She enjoyed herself there beneath one's mouth. Each word knocks another of the remaining teeth out of my head. What grows back are incisors, every one.

One wishes one had a vision. Has one mentioned this before? A vision to be recorded in this fictitious journal, using a fine fountain pen made of real fountains. Semi-real, in any case, as a semi-erection.

BITE ME BITCH!

I scream at me. But what I scream really is just:

BOX

I don't think I mean by that word:

PUSSY

I just mean:

BOX

I hope. Semi-real, in any case, as a semi-erection, though why am I thinking of that again. Why?

In my hands there is a box: gold lid, black walls, white hole.

I open up the box.

I'm old.

I have the heat of someone rushing in my midsection and there is all this colored chalk stuffed in my skull, teeth of pudding against pudding.

I swallow what I can.

Between my legs there comes the ripping and a little shower of white rocks. The rocks have cities cut into their small heads.

I run, stumbling, hearing guns, no longer laughing, doing nothing.

The rocks continue to shit from me until they do not and I can breathe.

It is interesting in this way how history is about things though not necessarily about the things that are interesting in the time of the original history or rather the original history, if history is only a thing that exists in the present, is made of the thinking things interesting that were not necessarily thought interesting at the time the history is built upon. On the other hand, it is also interesting that the things that are not thought interesting are the things upon which the ideology that will become history or is, that is to say, or is the stuff dreams are made of, if dreams are had, is never interesting at the time, that is to say, now. For example, one is thinking of an example this instant, and one can assure another one that it is not interesting in the least.

I am no longer holding any box, but I have fingers, and on each finger there are rings.

On the next landing, long like the last one, but bright yellow, is another waiting box. It sits there looking at me with its corners, these ones yellow. I can hear the underbuzz, and I am creaming.

I leave the land alone, though well beyond the box there is a window through which anything could be.

I creep onto the next flight, going backwards, watch the watching box watch me. These stairs' heads are hair covered and have holes you cannot read about. They fit my foot good. I love them. I get caught up in one and start to think about forever. I want to eat the middle from my own meats a lot. There is so much lively stink time. I hurry up. The steps are kind of wider where I want them to sit still and sometimes when I cannot get a leg up I have to roll wholly over and make a hump. My slit seems to fit around the stirrup of the steps' bent even when it tries to crush my sacs. Heavy grapes in my lovehandles wanting puncture and getting none.

At the second instance of a window I pause a second to look out. I am afraid to see head on into the something so instead I look good at the wall, and with the corners of my peep see what against the grade and grain I can clean see. Down there it looks regurgitated, the neon plates strung into foam and sopping all against the scourged face of the ocean, a mussy muppet of a life. Still, in the glop some bodies appear spinning. They do gyration in the mink. Spines and haircuts and postures folded, even from my great direction overhead. Some of the bodies in their glowing make special language to say hi to me up here, coagulating briefly like shit at magnets and then disrupted again by the blow. Where there used to be the many other towers I cannot see any of them there at all. Peelfish, stinky bodies, accidental life. I punch the glass. My hand breaks and leaves woowoo on it, streaked in the manner of a wishing person. I cough up needles. Cough up more bodies. Cough up a pool in which I swim. I am again walking up the stairwell and then still stays by my side. I still will not look. I still see anything I want.

Remember. Predicate absence. Good stuff. So the psyche's a one-liner. Such surface is slick for skating. Is it a wonder one is alone. One dreamt once of Theodor Morell, though one didn't know him personally, and in the dream he didn't wear glasses and was known by intimates as 'Honi.' Such luck. By oneself, one would do most anything for a chance to be nicknamed Der Spritzenmeister. That was his name. Though one would introduce oneself as Emil. Leaving off the consonance. Leading one to the sudden realization that there's necessity behind. Invention is what is meant to be said.

[○]

Somehow I am running.

I have the blue job in my purse. Folded sweetly in the tuck of me. Why? Until the Late Middle Ages it was not apparent to contemporaries that there would be, or could be, two different and competing legal systems in England. Why? It makes me stoop. I wish I had my helmet back. To stoop harder. The steps are orange.

There is the box: bigger than a Screaming Machine, smaller than a hole. I stop and think and look and wonder and the box begins to walk. Its backend scrapes against the power and tremors through every inch of everything.

I close my eyes and walk till I am gone.

[○]

Commit to memory: in American law, discovery is the pre-trial phase in a lawsuit in which each party through the law of civil procedure can request documents and other evidence from other parties and can compel the production of evidence by using a subpoena or through other discovery devices, such as requests for production of documents, and depositions.

In other words, discovery includes

(1) interrogatories,
(2) motions or requests for production of documents,
(3) requests for admissions, and
(4) depositions.

Uncommit. What one would like to do mostly is spend a night in a museum. It's been a dream since childhood, to spend a night in that house of dreams, that wishing-well that comes complete with café and gift shop. The gift shop being like those nuggets of dream-truths within dreams, letting one know what are those things within the dream-house worth attending to, that gilded spectre of one's mother not one's mother that is one's truest mother, being that ruby-red wish for alterity, as if. Sir John Fortescue was of the opinion that anyone who came forward to volunteer to give testimony in a case should be tried for maintenance, since he should have waited to be issued a writ of subpoena. If it were not for the undestined postcard or the framed miniature poster or the thematic tote, it would remain a mystery one what one wants. A mystery that bears repeating. If there's anything one could imagine, it's repetition. The old call and no response, regular as a heartbeat. Like chickens, that is to say, clucking along in tireless respiration. One has taken up reiteration, or mean to, again, it's a difficult thing to begin but endlessly easy to continue. Like poetry itself, it has no particulars but the bits left out. Like another one. Commit to memory: under the law of the United States, civil discovery is wide-ranging and can involve any material which is relevant to the case except information which is privileged, information which is the work product of the opposing party, or certain kinds of expert opinions. (Criminal discovery rules may differ from those discussed here.) Electronic discovery or 'e-discovery' is used when the material is stored on electronic media. Uncommit. Sir Thomas Smith commented that the jury system in the time of Elizabeth could not exist without the ability to compel testimony using the writ subpoena. Commit to memory: in practice, most civil cases in the United States are settled after discovery. After discovery, both sides often are in agreement about the relative strength and weaknesses of each side's case and this often results in a settlement which eliminates the expense and risks of a trial. Uncommit. At this time, maintenance was viewed as the primary evil of the legal system. Commit to memory: political songs of the day evoked the problem: 'At Westminster halle (*Legis sunt valde scientes*); Nevertheless for hem alle (*Ibi vincuntur jura potentes...*); His owne cause many a man (*Nunc judicial et moderatur*); Law helpeth noght than (*Ergo lex evacuatur*).' Uncommit. The unsaid. There's so much that one could not say. One withholds legions, continents. If one started not saying all that one could not say, there'd be no end to one's ongoing. One would become non-loquacious as the day is not long, the sun would not set on the lack of one's spoken horizon, one would be an inspiration for the many who do not become and those who would not be. The unsongs sung about one. Safe to unsay, one might rally untold millions not to the mountaintops, one would have no dream of one day, no dream worth not telling, one's privations would be the stuff of no legend, and one'd unfill the history books with no account of one's undoings. This would be a kind of brilliance of the kind one is quite capable of. In the manner. Of which one is capable. Say it again. It occurs to one that one has not yet set out what one means not to say, having become preoccupied by the not saying in the first instance. It could be pointed out that it's not for lack of trying. Nor, if the truth be told, by any form of distaste or desire. And desire, mean to say. In fact, as they say, one would put a paw on a stack of and swear to that one's lack of saying is entirely the cause of oneself. Discovery. Say it's so. Swear. This is what makes it Biblical. The strictness with which the courts interpreted the laws against maintenance was an expression of the censure of the common law. Causal. Thought equaling deed. One is very theistic in this fashion. It is a fashion, doesn't one think. Doesn't one, that is to say. A uniform would be nice. Would befit one. A style, like a certain cut or false fur, or a belief in Hissown. Private, in other words. Still. Encore. One nonetheless has an itch to see the seaside but not by the sea but from the side of the sea, the other side of seaside, the sidesea. This was impossible. Proved impossible. And yet inevitable. Not unlike the movement from metamorphosis to metaphor, or the proliferation of soft black metal. But the censure, overall, proved to be ineffectual. One has taken to following the careers of others with increasing concern, as in them one detects a bit of oneself, not the public bits, of course, but the more private, those parts kept surrounded by small hairs and other adorable knick-knacks of detail. These are the kinds of movements that betray one, or the other, to be exact, for they're the ones one is able to track. Liable, mean. Always liability in saying. One thinks of setting up a blog to this effect, or perhaps another. Maybe a twitter feed. Maybe a planned twitter feed. Maybe an idea about a plan for a twitter feed. There will have to be some time spent thinking about the homepage design. And the preference for character over content. Apple-scented, like the side of the sea.

[○]

At the third landing, dogs are on. Circles of them. I believe they make a pentagram. I am compelled to step into its center. When I do, there is a purr. A pumping underneath me and on both sides both at once. I'm starving, I'm swearing. A nodule descends from the ceiling and I take it in my ear. Can feel it droning through my mind, my own pillars and cerebrum, for which the tower too makes pools. A shine of rinsing offered at my underbelly booming milk up to clean my pate and make me feel happy while I'm taking the cold fusion of the nodule's foodgift down into my body.

The dogs watch me go and go. They whimper somewhat in their dogtummies, wanting all of what I got before they could get it. Their wanting makes me want more. I take what I inhale. I swish it around in my beanhead. I get it. I feel my sets of systems purring with the purring. My ten thousand nipples. I am tired. I stand up harder. I am good.

Soon my belly is so descended I can't lob it off the floor. I'm dragging it around all underneath me without even moving. I hear the stairs. Hear them going on without me and I have to hurry up. Several daschunds batting at my toeweb. A Doberman rubbing his skull frame at my ridge. I can't help it. Look at me sagging. Look at my huge butt.

I shoo the dogs by screaming but they don't go anywhere. Ten more come stick their muzzle in my new moves. Another nodule comes down out of the light, which has refolded several ways to make another symbol, my lids so fat I cannot see. The food tastes like porcupines and rebar, the fortunes of cookies, waddle chafe. Damn, it's my colitis.

More dogs. Mange dogs. Gold dogs. Wolf snarl. Shitting. It gets intense. Snouts and paws and pumping and another nodule and the floor and the stairs not stopping and my big guns and my pudendum being turned quite inside out from all the cells that I have asking and my butter baby smile.

When I have become so large I have no legs or elbows altogether, the dogs begin to roll me down the floor. They nudge me goodly with their best sides. Some of the remainders hoot an anthem—as not every dog can touch me. I am feeling misconstrued. A globule.

I am a perfect sphere.

Sometimes one becomes tired of whispering. After all, there's no one. Mustn't say. Say nineteen-sixty-eight. Say battery. Say the truth. Who was it that said numberless are the world's wonders, but none more numbered than man. It bears remembering. There are so many things to remember. More not to be said. They'll get nothing more from this one. More of nothing that is to say. Not saying. Not yet. Not yet time. What one would like. The other day, one remembers it distinctly, one was thinking that one should take a page from history and do something. The problem was, as it is recollected, that one felt the constraint of history itself, that is to say, there were so many things to do, at least potentially, that one felt stymied by the lack of historicity to direct one's actions. Meaning attention, since by actions were bound to be historical in anyone's estimation. Which leads one to a contemplation of bonhomie, in the broadest sense. Some people think one is less than forthcoming, but one thinks they mistake one's natural reluctance to disclose with a lack of geniality or simple good-heartedness. One wishes to correct this misimpression, which one believes is due to an etymological misunderstanding, or rather an overstanding, something architectural in its dimensions and ambitions, which, again, if one can be honest with oneself, at least privately, is the root cause of history itself. Say forty-five. Say obey one's elders. Say respect. Say slimming. Toothless. Say again. There was an effort to end this practice by providing punishment to whole categories of professional testifiers, such as serjeant-pleaders. This reveals the itch for the metaphysic. The epic. The metric, that counting-cause of the poetic. One believes it was Wednesday that someone said something in passing about poetry being a matter of meter or of other numbers, loosely grouped. Like chickens, though one might be mistaken in this.

"It is the best day of my life," I'm wheezing, through the fat around my speaky hole and the center of my center spinning. In my spires the meat uncomes collapsing and sitting down on pockets of itself like houses into drudge. The numbers of my nipples raining sour and then electric white gunk from my chest, in trampolines that spill and invert and shoot to shower from the night in shifts of the greatest want I've asked out of me via the friction and the pressure so many hours humped up against a bump of flesh or in my sigh, the filter of the large vent in my innards from what I've sucked up or eaten or lived near laughing in the rhythm of the baby with no forward or behind. I need nothing here. There is leisure in the sunning of the ball. The dogs around me are a pudding. The pudding of my reason. Forget this. Thou shalt have no other god before one. Ergo: So many other gods. Proof in pudding. Proof in glass bottles. Gods in glass bottles. Wrong gods. Wrong bottles. I don't remember any weekend. I am at three desks at once in my ibe sphere becoming flattened, stunned dimension, purpled pillows of the sweat where through the pistons of my chickenheart I hear the outside with me also leaning sucked to center, rashed and buzzed like who am I, though where on my rind against the blood the outside touches I get spitty. I white out: colored soft into the nothing of nothing, the bubble of my grunt, whose, and in the no part of the nothing there is silence, windows, and in the rest part of all the rest I taste disease: my cleanest bloodcells coming crumpled and ejaculating something darker than my million nipples through the three holes of my moneyprism and the blenders of my eyes and my foodspout still caught in the syllabism of one long chanting sewing my last lesions to my teeth and with the gathering of the mass becoming so thick there is no ground here, there's no glisten, until with the mud I am the ground and so I am.

[○]

One who wishes to see a perfect hole must imagine. One imagined oneself once, once, that is. The other day, was it, one was thinking to oneself, for one would not have it any other way; one has tried thinking to others and there's nothing in it but heartache. Heartache and a good stiff one. Two severed things that go great together.

One has drawn a chalk outline around one's whole self, extending a bit up what would be otherwise considered a wall and a bit down what would otherwise, depending on the p-o-v, be deemed either a ceiling or a bit of armpit. One has named it the other, which I pronounce as though it rhymed with Doug, and one is determined to get through this together.

In the match, soon, I can insist, and so I will: I am in and against every inch of dirt, mirrored in the grip of land to air above me by the dogs having bristled up to fill all air.

The human earth, a rind of dog meat kissed against the skin and skin and skin of me.

Anything I say aloud here spurts.

Pyramidal sponge holes. Blowing.

Each of the human dogs possesses a vagina and a cock. There are numerous references indicating that there had developed a class of professional testifiers, quite apart from lawyers and advocates, who could be purchased to testify in jury trials. The point being that one is only superficially. That's the fact of it. Not skin, skin's easy, skin's a false separation, easily vent. One exists on a deeper surface, the one not-one behind the eyes. One are mean. Only at the surface. The dogs begin to fuck themselves in the rhythm of the grains of America burnt and grown and burnt again, and fed into the big beef patties and wedged against the big beef patties on the lacquer table where whose chubby hands would rub. The dogs making rub-warmth to warm the lather between us and rise from each inch of me small cities in the image of the center building, thin as me. Night, at the center's center, riding down in one throng-lipped elevator with the suction of the copulation, the sheaths and lips making a rustle that rises bridges on the meat along the inseam of my nose.

Where the cities hit the dogs they crush the dogs. The bones gone mush make music that become the celebration music. The ribcages are the taquerias. The colons are the doormats to the newsrooms where the word will be printed on pink skin. Six dogs from every hour in the smother of rutting.

In each city bursts six cities, piling up in HVD. Men with Berettas fill a grandstand in the great room of the centermost apartment in each one, olive-skinned men firing their lungs out through the squealing ceiling. One hair grows connected to the navel of each from each, threading the cities, bringing power to the bedside tables and the burning lengths.

In my mud I'm rasping. A bed of tanning lengths of sexflesh in my saddles, a bronzing leather burped over my face. A mask I'll wear to dinner at the buffet inside my kidneys as they billow underneath and work to lick the runny off the screens my liquids passed through in replicate and so unwind. I get the chalky flavor in my mouth and then am hissing with the spittle in my largesse. This elbow node opens a butter prism underneath the sunken pasture where the child Jesus is said to have been born, and in the flowing bruise-cream from the gesture I feed myself another week: six days blinked in the duration of a good bite of a biscuit, which is both me and never me.

Actually, one spent most of the other day making vacation plans for when it's all over, and the other kept bringing up the seaside, when the one knows how that makes the other feel, and one kept mentioning mountains, which made some weep at the invisible. Sublime, one would sob, until one could barely stand to think of any kind of breakfast, even Continental. Where must some be going? Increasing strictness against corruption of all kinds at jury trials made many reluctant to testify. One has taken it upon oneself to pretend as if there were an exit. As there now is, as one must know.

In the bilge my back breaks around my spine and lets the burst out. It fills in around the blooms with what I've ate. A pasty syrup-colored innard-incubated and slopped off, into the cracks wherein the earth has allowed tunnels rubbed out from the divots, each also bursting into ten. Veins of ore of buttered okra, candy pillows, seams of curd of pastry, corn. Corns around my ankles from the gyrating inside my where my tendrils turn to mush too. "Mmm, I love to taste me," someone whispers in my ear.

One has taken it upon oneself to prove there is an existence. Inside the helmet I am nothing. I have the constellation mind: in which the points of light are no longer funded to the firmament but to some slick black animal named Shitface. I'm getting built. Getting hammered in my hammer section, which can take more than I meant. As there now is, as someone must know. What one is missing is a sense of organization, or what could be considered an agenda, particularly the kind that coddle, by which one means cradle, in copious leather notebooks. I look down at the calcium and conditioner of where my gut used to bubble out before me and see the language written on my balm of meat:

OUCH OUCH OUCH OUCH OUCH OUCH OUCH OUCH OUCH
OUCH OUCH OUCH OUCH OUCH OUCH OUCH OUCH OUCH
OUCH OUCH OUCH OUCH OUCH OUCH OUCH OUCH OUCH
OUCH OUCH OUCH OUCH OUCH OUCH OUCH OUCH OUCH
OUCH OUCH OUCH OUCH OUCH OUCH OUCH OUCH OUCH
OUCH OUCH OUCH OUCH OUCH OUCH OUCH OUCH OUCH
OUCH OUCH OUCH OUCH OUCH OUCH OUCH OUCH OUCH
OUCH OUCH OUCH OUCH OUCH OUCH OUCH OUCH OUCH
OUCH OUCH OUCH OUCH OUCH OUCH OUCH OUCH OUCH
OUCH OUCH OUCH OUCH OUCH OUCH OUCH OUCH OUCH
OUCH OUCH OUCH OUCH OUCH OUCH OUCH OUCH OUCH
OUCH OUCH OUCH OUCH OUCH OUCH OUCH OUCH OUCH
OUCH OUCH OUCH OUCH OUCH OUCH OUCH OUCH OUCH
OUCH OUCH OUCH OUCH OUCH OUCH OUCH OUCH OUCH
OUCH OUCH OUCH OUCH OUCH OUCH OUCH OUCH OUCH
OUCH OUCH OUCH OUCH OUCH OUCH OUCH OUCH OUCH
OUCH OUCH OUCH OUCH OUCH OUCH OUCH OUCH

What color. On my skull, a portrait of two needles sexing each other's' eyes and laughing with their skin. Red would be nice. Or yellow. Scrape the surface. Discover it is all surface. Whereas by now above the cities have swelled out cities have grown crystal sternums in their hearts, see-through statues in the center of the cities' center, a body with no head, in my own mind I am chocolate and can taste myself becoming melted under cold bone. The slick rosary of my reduplicative aorta announces my father's name while playing Taps, its notes shot down the plastic cylinder of the curlicue straw I have pushed out of my biggest pore, which by matter of cause is the pore in my forehead, and the dogs go on and do more sing. The dogs have been at this receptacle before. The cities six high, thirty-six high, whatever is thirty-six times thirty six, but in my mind I hold no math now but by counting cells becoming ice cream, putty, becoming rats' bones slurred on mine. And in them the mirrored cities upon cities where I'm pressed against impending into receptacles of miniature disease: loosing my teeth, beating my hair out, darkening my blood, putting the putty in my lungs where I had needed, scraping the reason from my sticky surface, removing any idea of who I'd been or known or loved or wanted or been inside of or been in full. Root beer up my butt and laughing ashes in my wallop. Scrape below, discover the nothing that bleeds. See what is bleeding. One wishes. There was a concern in these institutions that law be congruent with natural moral law. Red would be nice. Or yellow. The happier colors, those that lend themselves well to balloons and the glut of satisfaction when I am upside down and so are the cities and we're making one another into AHHHHH.

The dogs sound like black metal and have the fuck of Mahler, the peel of something thrown into a pit, the bob of judo, the piercings of mall punk born again. In their punt the lyrics lash in scissor-rhythm to line my insides with bright patties, which up close looks portal-colored and I eat it and I'm through: through the window of my cerebrum and laughing at my rash, from where all the rashes ever have come over and ground their knees in to camp out.

In my flesh the rashes watch a movie. It is the movie of my life. I would not know.

I try to laugh and tell the story in voice-over but all that comes out is my mouth: the tunnel of my lungs extended teeth-first into soda, sunrise, shitstain, dogs for miles. Over the course of a generation or so after 1215, the jury system began to be rationalized and regarded as a judicial body, a judicial body, a judicial body. Parties or their counsel were presenting facts and evidence to the jury. Court of Equity grew out of the Court of Chancery, which were controlled by the Church.

The mush. The mush of me and anybody. The mush of sun too far, cords long strung from my palate and gum meat to the bubble of the center of this meat, which in its extension ejected from me is the tower, is the junk, and in the light of me I can walk along me and feel my legs squish in my fat hugs, and feel my language made a pasting of the ideas of the night. One last and everlasting. Heavy bumped like my uterine wall, or the indentations on my glans. The lighter I walk the deeper my feet reach, gluing ashy putty to my bumps.

In this way, the great concern was equitable justice or 'equity.' I said 'in this way,' and one meant that as well. In fact, one can stand here now in full dress and insist that all of it is stuffed with meaning as a homing pigeon with mites. Non-existent, except for the mites, but one can't have a parasite without the predicate situation, or at least this is how the math works out. Which is the key to my exeunt, if one can use such an anachronism. If one can, which one can, being wholly anachronistic as all are, given that all will not have been. Not yet. Never yet. That's the beauty of typeface, isn't it. Font seeming so factual. Even sans serif, though it doesn't read with the same basso authority. Avec serif, then, like gutters around a whorehouse, it's the orderly movement of the structurally obvious we're after. Syntax, in other words. Where was one? Mathematics. It occurred to one that if one's situation can be said to be that of an aggregate, and that must be conceded, or one will get nowhere, and why not, given the *a* then *b* then *c* of phenomenology, at least as experienced relative to indigestion, if the aggregate applies to the state one is in, then the contrary must be equally, and one might see how the terminology is quite helpful here, as anywhere, really, give someone a dictionary or even a thesaurus, and one might make a whole man out of the other or any number of spare parts, if the contrarily is equivalent, mano a mano, right, then reversal is in order. Subtraction. The take away. The withheld from the withholding. The subpoena developed as a creative writ, the 'writ subpoena', from the Court of Chancery. One was once in a small boat with a hole in its bottom, or one had, and one would have drowned, or one would, had it not been for the principle of mathematics at play. Algebra being no one's fool, maintaining that the addition of any set of variables, no matter how well equipped with rubber boots or the justification. The amazing thing was to see the principle of the urge itself.

Look at the glass crammed in my mind, its defended rooms stuffed from the inside with the dust and flat of days, maggots crammed like peanut butter to the rooms on rooms I know somewhere in here I have walked, I can tell by the smell of me still lingered, condom water and body wax, stamp glue and someone barfing. It's me barfing. I am me. In the guggle of me I cannot keep me in me even nothing, my holiest holes itching to be filled among the juggle of these sacs' balls and the holes inside those still. I roll. I boom and barf and make me giddy, gerbils flying, baby teeth, a box of candy gelled to sugar, a picture of my stomach, a candle of the length of my intestines, loose matches, inkless pens.

Inside the cities made to mushing on the far side of mouthy light I hear inside the buildings in the buildings the better people getting old. The stairwells sizing in the mix around the center to the nothing where in my body's body I am caught and colored rising in the rising. Saying words I've said before again aloud. Calling for someone to come get me at a volume only I can hear, worn and wanted, growing larger, creamed up in the puff. Each of my hairs big as my whole life. My whole life big as the shunt in fifty plastic tunnels rising into one floor, glazing out as ice beneath my feet. Watch me walk into the fortune. My deflections. Watch me watch me want.

[○]

At the top floor of the central column I find a prism shaped like I am.

The celibacy around my prism's neck has grown into a forest where the mites borne in my neck has colonized and cried, slicking the center of my chest to gleam in mirror to the column's milky sheath.

The shaved bush of the prism reflects the lightest lathe of light, the shake of circus barkers screaming prices for my organs to the beetles in my knees. The gleam is a malfunction, I remember, as there is never any light.

The color of my helmet is distinctive though I cannot recall of what.

The rope is wrapped around my neck. I am tied to someone just above me floating, wide as the whole sky, though the clear walls of the central column cut it off, and outside it, it goes on.

Someone keeps jerking on the rope from the far end, tugging out a code. A double. A judicial body. A secret society. A double. If I could remember any letter long enough to hold the next one I could spell the words, and instead the birds come leaking, pulling down the color of the sky: white then white then whiter then out of any reach of mind, as in the way a skin becomes indented it owns not any name at all.

In endless sight, one has been keeping one's voice a secret all this time, when now one knows that it is one's way out.

Out.

The other was thinking earlier. The other was thinking earlier that what the other meant to describe was that ineffable feeling of cold when one has been very badly burned. And the corresponding feeling of heat as one freezes to death.

[○]

I have to know how to get back here when I am done with wherever else there is.

One has to know how to get back here when one is done with wherever else there is.

[o]

What I want (or I imagine): my hands in tremble, ever puking. Skin pouring off the knuckles for the fire.

What I am up against (in rungs): six walls, one on each side, inside the silence of no dogs barking, sheath to sheath, sent to skin in skin again so thick there is not even nothing, there is none.

What I have: a gun up my urethra, down my esophagus, in both my ears, one trigger on each finger, nozzles in nostrils, butthole plugged.

And yet I cannot: stop shitting, the liquid pouring out of me into the light, and there beside, the prism sluicing such a heated stream there is no white. No color in the nothing but the humming of the rising steam and sizzle of what gushing, not come or urine, but more meat.

Why I know any of this: because I'm hungry, because there is someone in me upside-down, playing the stone keys of my colossus, calling new name after new name. Each name reiterated slides from my mouth into the light punching up glass panels over old air cubing in my body and my prism shaped like me.

[○]

In the bend and collision of the panels. There are several towers now. In each of the towers there I am beside me barfing, ramming my bumpspot against the ground trying to want, and want, or more so: my skin inside me eating my skin. The floor of the top floor of the column underneath me makes a moaning like getting snipped, filling up with its own infants, floors on floors.

Through the prismatic glass of my name towers I see the cram of cities scrunched below in the pig meat and of my body so crammed in mass there is nothing of them but old ash.

This was not always seen in the common law courts, which were more pragmatic, and were concerned mainly with land law and inheritance. Maybe seventy-three. There's no butter no soft cheese no warm scented white bread, nothing, there's nothing. What one is trying to say, and doing a good job of it, one will be the first to admit, for one has no false pride, having no pride at all, is that one had figured out a way out, a mathematical way, a way by virtue of the twin virtues, of the law of cause and equal effect, of the way of once a thing is done, it must be undone as well, just as warmth implies its lack, crunchy invokes chewy, the thought of a winter's day seems like a long hot summer afternoon.

The snow stinks like my skin. Can smell it ripping in the flutter, each infant edges circumcising the texture of the air inside the light leaving in its tunnel streaming of clear blood on the cities of nowhere. The blood, too, bunching through my tattoos and, too, rising wet pillars of thick red through my circumference to spell the words upon me here in 3D and in the image of me here beside me 6D and in the glass recreations D uncountable or at least not countable from where I am or at least not inside someone as lazy and old as I am where in the push of cut light through the window and my chest stretches and my double's doubles stretch and we make mush, the uncylindrical towers in our tower crushing up the air until inside the air the air is one. One red air of sick potatoes all chalky, undercooked.

Until the Late Middle Ages it was not apparent to contemporaries that there would be, or could be, two different and competing legal systems in England, one of them common law and the other equity. Five, at most. As was being said, one had deduced quite algebraically that if there was an aggregation, there would necessarily be its counter-gesture, which would prove most liberating. At least in theory, but what else does one have. One meaning the other. What one is thinking is that if one eats as much as possible, this will cause one to, in the manner of equilibrium, shrink. Gluttony will emaciate. Emaciation is emancipation, as all the sixth-formers know. One could start with a bucket of slop, drenched in syrup, and move on to something substantive thereafter. Lately one has noticed an itch for sweets. Not to eat, not necessarily. The smell of sweet. Found along the innermost and the fold just there. Where one would put the children, if one had any, making sure they were ill-prepared. Everything one has learned, one has learned from being ill-prepared. That, and at the point of an objective stance on the matter. No matter. One believes one was saying something about a one-legged man on a bicycle, in the unripped slits of the procedure. The writ having been written in the blood again I swim again inside the tower for the night—though there is no night in this hour, there in the prisms, under blood. In the swim of mesh even not seeing I feel my ten thousand partitions calling, cloaked. I bump my oatmeal arm against a pivot and spill more spill into the leak. My blood is blood for hours in the stairwells here convened. I breathe me back into me. In my breathing, light, I mind. Breaststroke and dog paddle where what seems upward, toward something, even still, though in my head the itch is all directions and anywhere I go is veal. Dead yards, dogs, or costumes: I wear them in my teeth. In the unripped slits of every dinner where nothing has been ate.

Remember this: The purpose. What is required. A spoon made of something else. A mother who cares. Nine o'clock in London. *Sept heures en ville. À quelle heure* my ripe red ass. They were, however, aware of the conflicting courts. No such thing. As one was saying, a one-legged man on a bicycle was riding by as one was eating a ripe red apricot.

In the mush I feel a ringing again. Please not the ringing. The tower's holy bell. Its tongue cut from the pudding of the babies underneath layered in my wombs and my testicles, great, my unbrothers, their unsistered wombs too scooting flues, sure, firing their guns inside as more wanting which owns every tower of every name. The bell bubbles my laughter, please no laughter, tickles more me out of my me than I would like. In dieting, in this manner, I can swim higher. The bell rubbing right, yes. There just like that. The harder I swim to climb the bell rings wetter, stirring the machines in my feet.

Underneath the dogs are swine. From their golden hair and bristle of the bark lining their bellies, the oinking comes in hoard, corkscrew tails plugged up to some soft ceiling as everyday as any breath, electrified and squealing, saying nothing, gone again. The blood is pigs and gone again and there are horses, skronking shit, doing the lift-kick into nothing to launch block of bricks of nothing at no sky. There is the tower, me inside it, me of me, yes there is nothing else, yes, in the mutation of this evening, sure, ok then, but the roiling of no meat. As what is not is is. And I.

In the silences between the bell.

In the silences between the bell I am more scared than ever and swim faster with the roof rushing in my rising for my skull. Its want eclipses mine inside the rising of it, I can feel it rising before I rise, can wish its impact sooner shooting cities through my cities made to none, these questions peeling out in pummel.

My grunting stirs the columns. The glass unsalading in oh yes again oh yes. Saying answers to the color's questions of questions in bright upswim. The bell unforevered underhead. My skin not its tattoos. My tattoos not my skin, and the word in word, the worming raining through the blood as nettle, air.

OUCH

Bloomed from the nettles (bloomed from my blooms unknowing (*I did not write this sign…*)): the tower again, crushed and falling, again, in the tower, yes, all in and over me, two different and competing legal systems.

Bloomed from the towers (in my wanting (*by now I am upside down made right side up*)): no tower but the tower clogged in me higher, roughing up though in the leagues below snowed in inverse to the inverse snow outside the wall. I hear the films of me of me caught in the speechglass screaming nothing, saying anywhere we've been, back to the first word of this collision and in the other house where words were writ: destructed and unstructed, what stink of vinegar in my lungs and on my thighs. As for the bumps that have been raised, they seem benign and, sure, will resink again or will fester and grow, become a room; and in my other her here's room too, a kind of snowing, or the light through or not through any hole or child, as I have heard her in certain hours saying there shall be no light here but through false boxes, inside boxes, and I too am a false box, and in my boxes, boxing, another ringing: sight of sight.

What the sight sees (shit, I'm slipping, the current recursing in my talk spots (*but I must go*)): white doorways, which hold buttons, which when pressed eject the rhyme, which filter through the mush of nothing coming nothing to explode into another rind with the lick of it insisting zippy around the tower in a milk growing a pink skin on its surface in the lurking so again I can look up; again I can see and hear the tower making wider, and I am every inch of every wall, and I am not the wall but getting nearer to the bell above the flux, where in the flush of me beneath me the suds are rushing up and sloshing in my something to be the curd on which I rise and am risen and the wet flooring bowing up on beds of blankets, overtired, sucked in no moonray to the moon beyond the moon, one fattened dome of nightlights hiding in the musk of nothing and of nothing against nothing but the burning, ouch, the burning sun, ouch, ouch, damn, ouchie, skin is screaming, but the voice is anyone's.

Any body (any hour (*none of this is mine*)): in the rush of flush I shut the door inside me and can see sun again, what luck. And as for every blink I'm blinking jewelry I see the baby of my mind, those pink curled rolled designed in quiet folded from the pygmies no finger of me ever held or hoped, instructed, or collared, puddled, or become thrown into a glee, burst to whine, wrapped and unwrapped and wrapped again and writhing, oceans under glass.

My fingers (Jupiter, Saturn, Isis, Locksmith, Bellum, Witch, Insissum, Silence, OAO, Gnat (*I did not offer any of these names*)): I feel them wrap around my throat for hours, even when I am no longer here. The tower pummels, rising into steam, until where around me I cannot feel me beyond the glass, the skyholes, and in my width of widths becoming softer I realize I haven't ever moved an inch or lied. My pink costume. My wedlock. Oooohhhh ohhhohhhho oohhhhh.

Inch (ash, collision, sentence (*suckholed, zeroed, presto!*)): in the rip I shake my hands. I hug me around my neck and shoot my piston. Replace the helmet. Stutter that. Where into the light globe of the tower's center's center through the hole of holes we call the floor.

[○]

Dog hole.

Skin around dog hole.

Skin around me around dog hole in long air.

Hair around skin around dog hole around center of tower shoved to fit to precipice in sick sky.

Docking no light. Tower having risen to the slur point of the posture of the city of the city of sick sky so once where I touch sky with my fur or lick of arms unraveled I can smell me spraying into space.

The space of walls. The meat of no meat around air surrounding cities in which one of many homes is my demolished home, in which I can still hear vibration of my bedroom orifice in which the bed has learned its mouth and can speak me through the rubble of the rubble of the no light, beg me back to rub my butt and cunt and balls against its blub a final time. To mate the bed with my unpeeling and gift the baby in its coils. A baby prison, like my body, though with slick of spit and retch and swear of years I've spread my junk across that mat in wicker charm.

In the air around the light around the glove of cities I am longer than a war. My nipples have no nipples, but the piercings glow like ice: to hold and giggle where the moons rub by intention from however many billion lengths over and away.

My scat tastes like magician, but I eat it with my eyes. I can't not, of all of me, and wide open, the tower in my spine, the spine punched in the pirouette of silent spinning under my fleshcorned compass constellationized.

Horse gloves. Skin to tongue. In the sadding sky I let my lick me and spew poodles of saliva through the ten fingers at a new glassy massive eye.

Through the slit of my two longest fingers I blow a breath and watch the wetting bend, the eye dilating along its quick seams into the round of more than else. Through the blooming eye I watch the lashing landscape of the dark suns spout no motion. I watch it warble in an anti-neon fright: not at what I am or hold or will be eating, but at the color of the round, their bulb caught in miniature eons rippled with the drunk I've swallowed year by year.

Glow dome. Lungs of my lungs. Skin not in the pushing, but the want. I spit a little laugh into the fruition and let the balloon bump with yearlings, their slow shit dripping down in spindles to the ground. The shit piddles in the myth of shit around the congealed cities where I no longer have my legs. No steps. No shush. In halving.

I cannot kill my face. Can feel the thump of my dumb pistons in the pull of cells over my cheekbones, gums, where in the spit I sit and ride. Outside me dark sees nothing but the sludge around us. Sometimes a single silent puff of smoke kissed to transmit in the mud of nowhere six directions, and six again, again. An infernal transmission. I have this darkened money up my slit.

In the refraction of my body through my body, the language comes out me in bone:

WHAT ARE YOU
WHERE DO YOU
THIS IS MY
GIVE ME YOUR

WHAT ARE YOU DOING UP HERE?

WHERE DO YOU THINK YOU'RE GOING?

OPEN

THIS IS MY HOUSE IN NO HOURS

GIVE ME YOUR OTHER ARM

Where I would reach I see the crystal clotting out the light. There is no light to not want in any body, and therein the pistons again become. Everyone is crashing. The lights make writhe. A beak. Around the body of the cities and the air and all the phrases, another house, another instance held oncoming in my teeth and beyond moan: not a tower but a whole sphere. I hear it listen. A house with no doors no locks no windows no width or ways at all.

[o]

One carved a model of one's mother's head from the last block one got. It was to size, or nearly, and did her more justice than the one previously composed of soap-bubbles and old snapshots of Plato. When one was a child, one summered in Goose Bay. One wintered in the distance to one's destination, for one was a simple people, always going here and there, and though Goose Bay was, in its mean and simple way, a place fit for the likes of us, one never quite fit in, having no habituation aside from a passion for nail-biting in theory and the smell of corn chips on one's shoulders in praxis.

In plural.

In weeping.

In suffering.

It was Hegelian, as one's mother used to say. It was unformed as a thesis, but everyone knew what was meant, and didn't, and did, and by then it was time to drain the marshmallows, roast one's whatsit by the memory of all that's holy, and go to bed. One slept in the top bunk, next to one's father, who held his bicycle to his chest most tenderly most of the night.

By 1350, the writ certis de causis (the 'writ for certain causes'), began having the clause subpoena routinely attached. As one was saying, there is something in utter nonsense that will allow for the slip of one thing to another, so that one might, in an exuberant moment of extemporanea, lose oneself altogether. This, too, is a mathematical certainty. For if the choice is—and it always is—between the all and the not-all, then invoking the all, or the call of the all, will most certainly provoke the not-all in response, leaving plenty of wiggle room in which to take one's leave. By, and one really feels one shouldn't have to spell this out, staying. One must admit to a certain modicum of organizational fidelity. Thus it becomes more and more apparent that in order to make a book that all might read, one must create a certain loyalty, penning happy songs, songs that vanish without a sound and songs that can be sung through a hollow reed. The writ quibusdam certis de causis is at least as old at 1346, and had subpoena attached. The great objection which common lawyers made to writs in this form was their failure to mention the cause of the summons. It is to be agreed that if one wants to meet, say a little girl without feet, or a little boy, who weeps and weeps, and suffers onto suffering, one begins not by showing the way out, that is to say, not by leading one astray, but by leading one in, through the fear, for there is fear, there is always fear, fear neverending, fear without fear, but fear standing just to the side, sucking in the gut, at, mean, sucking at the gut, no, in, that was correct, sucking in the gut, fear stands to one side and one must go through, being careful to brush as gently as possible.

It's impossible not to touch.

But to go gently.

It became the custom in the common law courts that the person would not be compelled to appear without having notice of the reasons for appearing. Early subpoenas carried no notice of the reason for the summons. That's the only hope for real subtraction. There is only the smallest opportunity. This must be remembered. One had forgotten, and all was lost. Objections in Parliament became loud and frequent. Luckily, a one-legged man on a bicycle rode by and put one in a mind for memory. Recollection, mean. The act of direction. Thoughtful as any liquid comfort one may have mentioned earlier. One may have. It remains to be seen. On the one hand, Chancery believed that wrongdoer might engage in maintenance to prepare the verdict before appearing in court. On the other, common law courts found it difficult to amend the presented writ, and many cases were lost for want of the correct writ at the beginning of the case. Still, if there's an out if there's an in—one can be certain as any other.

One should like to explain this further, but one believes it's time. Time and time again. Time for history, time for unmaking, time to put out the clock and wind the cat. Buckle, mean. One or the other has discovered something in all this. That there is a grammar to it. And once one has a grammar to it, why it's just a matter of parsing. And once it's a matter of parsing, then one has the freedom of the ancients. To, right. Too, as well. One wonders sometimes whether the weather and how come the simple declarative. One grew up among the simple declaratives. They were there, resolutely. In the manner of planned furniture. Shouldn't be rushing. Still. Should stay. Never again. Not to get through. Rather one should look at this in the manner of the Old West. Something with a stagecoach. A man named Kid. There must be horses, signifying horses. They are very much like trees in their metaphoric stasis. Being equivalencies, i.e. Das ding, or, if one might say, dash ding a derry dong, as one's mother used to say. Never was a woman like one's mother. There are places, to be certain, that are better than others, and some still worse than the ones next door, but there was a bastion about her that was indisputably unique. Absolutely, one might say if one were a person of faith. One realized the other day, most definitely a Friday, that while one was a person of belief, that is to say, a person who did, in fact, believe, proof of which was amply supplied by a nearly unconscious habit of bending at the knees when preparing to sit either in a chair or on the floor or, if one had a side of bed, there, at the bedside, and even if, one would imagine, by the side of the sea, one was not a person of faith. Meaning one ascertained the phenomenological sais quoi of the said chair, floor, hypothetical cot, mythical sea. Oceans of sea, such as written about in the history books. Which leads one to reiterate several themes, by way of synopsis.

The rolls of the medieval English parliaments contain numerous petitions and acts directed against the Council and Chancery. This is not a public endeavor. Never a public endeavor. Never endeavor. Never add when one might take away. Unlike umbrellas, there are these kinds of paraphenomenon that cannot be opened openly, though there is a small footnote about the indoors that applies equally. The other day one was pondering the problem of an aftermath and realized one had no attention, by which one means span. There's a kind of ribbon of focus, certainly, but not anything with the kind of width one could unfold across a muddy water, one with barges named Jessica R. or punters in orange shells or have families of four or more eat prawn sandwiches with mayonnaise by and then celebrate the eating with soft serve cones dipped in softer chocolate shavings. There's also the kind that fly from cathedrals, inside, often, outside to more structural effect, though one may be wrong about this, showing off for the neighbors. It occurred to the other that one mostly cathedrals for oneself, given the luxe interiors, as compared with one's friends to the farther East, who spend more effort on sizing, with more of an eye to the Big O, having no need for the first commandment, as there are no other omnipotents. To wit: call and response. The spirit of the Magna Carta, as well as some specific language within it, was the promise that justice in England to all citizens and their property would be in the common law courts, and nowhere else.

It's about medium, always. About mother, always, about message, always, about father, always, about always, always.

It is a cliché, and for this one can be congratulated, the hand, so to speak, primed like an antique well. There should be dependable chickens. Dependable in the sense of attribution. In 1331, these proclamations were again re-enacted. In 1351, they were again recited. One must have something to blame. Some fair thing to suspect. Guilt is everyone's ornament, everyone's sweet là-bas note. The King had to promise that the Council would not proceed without indictment of common law process on an original writ. To be a paragon of virtue is the happiness of vice—evil feeds on good, good on evil—it's the mutuality of ambush that is to be admired. Would, seeking its own level, meets would as like will call to any form of marked opposition. Presenting prime with its number. Unstained, unmatched, unfettered by praise or cheap condemnation, content with content, happy to be. Leading to the cleansing cultivation of great envy and the amplification of will.

One day, when a one-legged man on a bicycle rode by, one knew that one had seen one's father. It was ignored. Something that can never be moved or photographed. Something viewed through a hole. Something that is not a fixture, not a function, something that was less than the thing that came before, being the thing that came after what came after. Twigs, perhaps, a bit of gas, a touch of morning, a slap of frisson. In 1363, the command to Chancery was repeated by legislature. There was a proclamation that there be no original writs.

No original.

Writs.

No original writs.

I Utterance Three

The other body's spine, a cage inside a cage

OR:

Ununderstanding

[•/○]

One is most afraid of drowning. Or the drowning of those nearest and dearest. Nearest, anyway. One is less afraid of being found than of finding. That's not true at all, though one is uncertain if it's truer in reverse. One is constantly pulling at things to see if they are loose. Phantom teeth, for example, or missing limbs. A vestigial tail, not mine. One finds oneself mouthing air while falling asleep, as if chewing. Or at least biting. Off. Is one that literal. One is. The other, mean. One takes comfort in the stupidity of others, likewise their incessant breathing. Terror. Horror. The thought of bright meat.

I go on in.

I do.

I go into the house and close the door behind me.

The final house inside is pink: the pink of ash burned twice and smeared onto the face of a new child: thus, not pink, but the mask above it in negation; a color of a color set beside itself. One never wanted for anything but everything. One believes that if the artist is beautiful, no one will notice about the art. One believes in the abstract profundity of abstract profundities. One believes the less said the better.

Inside the final house there is a final house stuffed into the bread. I am too large to get in. The house around the house makes music where the houses touch most, squirting gold notes down the arches and the studs. The sound rides little rumps of worm down the hull under the house paint, coagulating in a white purse in the conduit of a removed attic mouth, sealed in from behind itself with more pink, of another nature, a slightly orangey tint of scoff.

These pronouncements were ineffective and ignored. Like things written on slips of paper and stuffed into almond cookies. Almond-flavored cookies. Almond-flavored cookies shaped like dying butterflies. Almond-flavored cookies shaped like dying butterflies cocooned in cellophane. Almond-flavored cookies shaped like dying butterflies cocooned in cellophane presented on a small square tray. Almond-flavored cookies shaped like dying butterflies cocooned in cellophane presented on a small square tray with an addition. A sign left in the final house on a platter set just beside the house inside the final house instructs me to remove my clothes. When I am naked I shall wash myself with my own spittle. I shall chew my nails down to the bump.

I do.

The addition. More legislation followed in 1389 and 1394. One sees one's point. Gestures towards the sensible. Toward the loss. The absence of. All to be found grammatically, i.e., in the manner of. One has given up an actual corporeal existence, that is to say, one gave it up. After finding that it didn't matter. All that matters is the scheduling of things. Sequentially. A priori. In 1415, the writ subpoena was denounced by name, as a subtlety invented by John Waltham. Another legislative act in 1421 called the subpoena not in accordance with due process. Lest the rest ask me to recite other bits of merit, the type that clings to the bottom of love, the part that lives ever after, farting along quite reasonably, faecal love, the kind that is best forgotten by others, who can't prove a thing worth proving. They've got nothing on the other. None of the goods. Not a one. By this time, the Council and Chancery were firmly established. Calumny. Secret Society.

I do.

The list is written in a thick hand, with a paintbrush, the pigment colored with the ripe scent of rippled shit. The color of the surface on which the writing has been printed is this color, too, yet I can read it. There is a trumpet in my hand. Small buds rise, too, in the calligraphy, which is gorgeous. A steady hand by a firm mind. The stalker of my stalker.

I blow the trumpet. I hear cats. Out of the trumpet comes another stretch of ugly paper. It says to smear the powder on my chest. There is a little packet of it for me hanging. I am to walk around the house: three times clockwise, three times counter-clockwise, three times clockwise there again. More power, on my lips and hair. The powder makes me appear aged. The trumpet's not there. There are candles, spindled, leaning, boned in from the roof. The low drip of their running strings a silence to the thrush of skins deciding. Calumny.

Calumny. One would inspire that, if one had aspiration beyond the old in and out, that constant humping of the god in one. On, mean. Forgive it. Never forget. One had a moment of inspiration, that urge to do more than just desserts, as if there could be more, but there could, one would imagine, one could imagine more. Hanging praise upon the dead, hanging the living till dead. Turning tricks with truth. Truth. That *faux ami*, when one knows good and well that it is untruth that proves the more faithful companion, the best friend. On one. On two. On ninety-four, in ninety-six.

What is left will be buried with one, though what's left will be only that which is permanently absent—the holes in one's teeth, the gaps and yawnings where once was the repeating organ. One will be more nothing than ever before. And they say one lacks ambition. They just don't know. One has got plans. Next on the list, nude, made of nothing, I see the list say to grow my hair down to my waist. This can be achieved, it says, by blinking, or by giving up what I have lost. And yet I cannot, in this house, close my eyes. I swing my fists at me to scare me and I am suddenly the bravest child, in glow. I blow the trumpet and feel my skin sing with it, and yet it never is enough. The songs already in me squeeze the sound out. I keep and keep them. I throw the trumpet on the ground. I scream at it just above it, my lips our lips.

Pinking.

My voice gets all over the floor. There are all these words that puke into the airlight and become suffered of it, zip up the seam.

I do.

Inside the house inside the final house inside the trumpet sound resounding I hear another of the me moan. The babies in the me inside the house inside the final house are moaning too. The babies in the babies in the me inside the house inside the final house take names, take wives and husbands, take the same breath all at once. Their cells flutter in fat packets through and through them to, in their blood, another sound. The sound squirts back into the babies into the babies around the babies into the house into the house into the house around the house around me.

My hair blurts to the floor. Soon there will be less of one and more of all the rest.

I have on the lipstick, the plum mask, the gauntlets, the money folder, the garter shirt. I am spinning with my linings end to end.

My blood is bigger than any other surface in this final house I am inside of and yet I fit into it well. My blood not blood but any evening, a long squatting, someone's dinner knife. Names come falling from me in warm water. Suds and blankets. Diamond malls.

The floor is bull. Secret Society.

To become nothing more and more, to be increasingly unfounded, unmanifest, unmanned. One will increase by one's plotted decrease until there will be more that is like than unlike, as the more one is finished, the more complete, and to be whole in absentia is an infinite proposition. Further legislation only encouraged these institutions. One of the philosophers said, and it's all the same which one, that there's nothing like real return to put one in a mind of finitude. Or the other way around. And the other way around. For there was a time when demoiselles meant something else altogether, a nice surprise for the ill-disposed or the uninformed. Today, having determined a way out via in and in and in again, for it is that time of year in which one may be beheld, that is, beholden, and once contemplated, may be set down again, forgotten, able to finally, that is to say, to get away.

The third instruction on the list on the platter on the floor in the final house says I am to remove the skin under my skin. By lifting the skin off via the clamp holes where the tattoo incisions have slicked down into a white mush in the house's hidden light, it says, I can raise by nails and teeth and wishing the overlayer, the cancered costume having covered and absorbed my laughing fright. The list recommends imagining a certain prior enjoyed evening during the lifting to redistract the frame, as there will be the hour of the screaming in my organs during this third and final final slight. And yet in the prism of my nothing there is nothing certain left to think. In the box of my head I feel the crush of cold computers and the tissues filled with snot. I look to lean beyond my skinself to seem something and cannot, there is no node, and so in the pinch and grapple of finding the skin plugs and the destruction of the web of webbing between my meat. There is only all around me every inch of all my speech vibrating the house inside the house, syruping the walls between these two with a milkbath while in the skin I raise and click. I hear the rummage of my tendons whorling while I pucker and serrate the skin under my skin with what I've got, which by now I'm sure is nothing but in the light there seems a knife. There seems from both my hands two blades big as a bathroom suddenly erected from my knuckles char, and in the grumbling of a second's second I hear the whole of me upchuck, no distraction. There is singing like some second canopy of birds, just right there in all that mudmeat, and in the same second's second the birds obliterate to musk. The musk rises in clean prisms in rollercoaster cars of ash under the leg of jackets where I pull and slice with what I have now and must become and in one magician's trick of tablecloth and dining set, a shudder, the pudding slip of someone slipping unseen into a room, I yank my underlayer up, out, through me and holding that curd shawl then and there then in the pink, in the pink house now, rather lighter, as my inseam itself is charcoal smooth, it has the light of something far off kissed within it and a rhythm of dented kites.

Like the leaves missing color, or rather just the one, then simply missing, still cling to the branch along with the lack of heat, or rather the cold, which clings steadier still, and the tree trembles and the leaves tremble but the cold is unmoved. As one is unmoved in one's own image, one's own imagination, though there are those birds in the back of the head that one once saw lined on some wire, black against some setting sky, cradled in the flit warmth of a yellow stop light. There were these birds, these skies, this cautionary night. One sees in oneself the end. Of oneself, and there's really no difference. A command dignified by the sanction of the law. A mandate lawfully issued under the seal of the court by a clerk thereof. After sunset fades on the Eastside, the other can go to the beach and pretend at blackless night. Soon there will be less of one and more of all the rest.

The rasp where I am in me there thereafter is draped and dripping overturned. I feel the air pouring down my arms in liquid horror, a delight like being eaten out while Waterboarded. I have bracelets around my wrist now. They are spinning. I have a little spinach in my teeth, between which my tongue is going splintered, dividing, redividing.

Three times clockwise, three times counter-clockwise, three times clockwise, once again.

Behind me in the final house where I came into it through the hole inside the final house's face there is not a door now but a small soft bottle placed on an indention in the wall. The bottle is full of white smoke, sealed in tightly. I do not see the bottle there. It is.

One sees the embers beneath the fire, it's quite metaphorical, this dying, this dying before dying, this desire for that narrow bed, cut to the quick of one's ambition. Width, where depth was wanted. Depth, where width needs be. There is nothing more terrible than the other. The plus one. And the lack thereof. Plus one, encore. Today is one's birthday. Requisites of form in the United States. It tears on cue. The list doesn't mention what to do hereafter with my lining draped over my fists, the knuckles shining through the pygmy fur size, little nibbled sections showing through, but in the light that rises from the house inside the final house, a cooling bean glow in great distinction to the glow up from my beat, along the skin I see the words upon it written, my spindling tongue pronounces each one out, and yet in the house I hear nothing, I see nothing,

I want nothing. I am on.

Wherein I read the words into me with my grease-eyes I feel nothing further past the quick of this topmost sudden skin, through which, in the bubble of the reading and speaking without seeing I begin to watch expand around me in balloon, the previously apparent organs and bone parts through my forum becoming puddled under, gobbed with air, in system of new gassing, inhalation, water, nothing, my skin in flags around my belly, neck, and knees. One hundred nations, squashed with cities, squashed with hovels, squashed with what I am.

Fétichise, déféticise et reféticise. And he knew also that the duty of all art lay in this sort of truth, lay in the self-perceptive finding and proclaiming of truth, the duty which has been laid on the artist, so that the soul, realizing the great equilibrium between the ego and the universe, might recover herself in the universe, perceiving in this self-recognition that the deepening of the ego was an increase of substance in the universe, in the world, especially in humanity, and even though this doubled growth was only a symbolic one, bound from the beginning to the symbolization of the beautiful, to that of the beautiful boundary, ever though it were but a symbolic perception, it was precisely by this means that it was enabled to widen the inner and outer boundaries of existence to new reality, even though these boundaries might not be crossed, widening them not merely to a new form but to the new content of reality which they enclosed, in which the deepest secret of reality, the secret of correlation was revealed, the mutual relation existing between the realities of the self and the world, which lent the symbol the precision of rightness and exalted to be the symbol of truth, the truth-bearing correlation from which arose every creation of reality, pressing on through level after level, penetrating toward, groping toward the unattainable dark realms of beginning and ending, pushing on toward the inscrutable divinity in the universe, in the weld, in the soul of one's fellow-man, pushing on toward that ultimate spark of the divine, that secret, which, ready to be disclosed and to be awakened, could be found everywhere, even in the soul of the most degraded B, this, the disclosure of the divine through the self-perceptive knowledge of the individual soul, this was the task of art, its human duty, its perceptive duty and therefore its reason for being, the proof of which was art's nearness to death, and its duty, since only in this nearness might art become real, only thus unfolding into a symbol of the human soul; verily this he knew.

Fétichise, défétichise et refétichise.

Someone is making sandwiches in my summerhouse, somewhere in there, someone with a hairbow and a mind. Someone in the basement of the basement of the beehive hung over a bassinette inside a tree. These windows pilled in both my nostrils, globular, in baste, both of which grown large enough now that the birds the house inside the house had hidden come pouring out of it and up my personal area. The birds and birds and pigeons and the color of their flap and the bees and strings of guitars dragged behind them, dragged up through me in my swell. There is the sound of a construction, a detonation in reverse, then trombones and someone coughing again, slitch of ribbons tied and tied, a dump of crystal sand.

Then, just as quickly, in the throttle, my center pulls my skin back down around me, a new purse. Curled in a tight, young packet of my body's body with the ham hocks of my extroversion laminated, the skin around my eyes curls in hissy bundles that trail around the corners where I look, coloring the final house off-color from its color, purple, yellow, then golding, greening, wrung. The web of index of the prisms is a Paint by Number of some translucent god, who I will not ask for money, or for forgiving, anyone.

Fétichise, défétichise et refétichise.

That art existed B oh, did it still exist, was it allowed to exist B only insofar as it contained pledge and perception, only insofar as it represented the fate of man and his mastery of existence, insofar as it renewed itself by fresh and hitherto unaccomplished tasks, only insofar as, in achieving them, it summoned the soul to continuous self-mastery, compelling the soul to reveal level after level of its reality, as, descending step by step, penetrating deeper and deeper through the inner thickets of its being, it gradually approached the unattainable darkness from which it had always surmised and been conscious of, the darkness from which the ego emerged and to which it returned, the dark regions where the ego developed and became extinguished, the entrance and exit of the soul, but likewise the entrance and exit of that which was the soul's truth, pointed out to it by the path-finding, the goldly-gleaming bough of truth which was neither to be found nor plucked by means of force, since the grace of finding it and the grace of the descent were one and the same, the grace of self-knowledge ,which belonged as much to the soul as to art, their common truth; verily, this he knew.

The house inside the final house looks enhanced also, vibrating seam by seam in the mesh of what it wants and all its inside singing. The cells pull up and open, a presentation. Guns. A yawning of the best kind. I put my finger in its bunch. I tickle, pull back and lick and make it glisten. I fit in my whole fist. My fist inside the house inside the final house feels as roach-covered, the feelers and the platelets seized around my knuckles and my length. I do a moan again and make it moan through me, combing the sliver wide enough to hide inside, and inside, the splay.

The time and place must be specified. What is that? Description, s.v.p. Certainly: the eyebrows were black, medium thickness; brown eyes, medium width, smaller vertically; wide nose, medium width lips, medium fullness; medium chocolate complexion; black mustache; oval shaped face. Looking at said figment, the graphics specialist noted he had a prominent nose. Not so. None of it. Have none of it. No matter. What one means to say. The other was blotchy with a sharp nose, sharper eyes and a small mouth, all crowded in the center of the face, huddled together in futile attempt at warmth. Not so. None of it. Again, i.y.w. Je veux la débâcle et sans attendre je ne tiens plus en place, mourir ou amortir la vie, i.e., it's life or death for me, aussi. Come now, that's the best you can do—question. Answer—again. Allons enfants de la Patrie, le jour de gloire est arrivé. In the American system there is a fundamental right to be heard in due process of law. Do say. Where did that other come from. From within, most certainly. Never the other. Sight contra sentiment, it's a cage match for the spoils of the imagination.

I do.

The splay in spray of something closing as it opens around me in milk fur with the shudder of something seasoned and giggled into and spilled upon. I hear the whir of video rewinding or in fast forward being torn, then when I can look again as coming in has closed my eyes I see the night. The night blooms in glue, a fortress, a bedroom, with the small smell and unseen drywall legwork of a mouse.

Inside the house inside the final house there is a painting of my eye. The eye is large as some blue billboard, cut with virus flakes and mush. My eye watches me come to stand before it. In my iris, that little roar: from some hole large enough to stick my head in. The meatflesh of the eye-white clings around my neck. I wiggle. I hear mushrooms. Inside my eye I cannot see.

Something screwing where my hair is. The hair twists. A beam of chocolate. My scalp erupting knotted, loosing mouthwash and pouring crème down my skull's sides. A special popsicle. An ash font, I think. I scream inside my eye and make me all wet with another wash of unclean snowing. I feel my history change my name. It has been and will be my name forever. I am giggling. My eye sucks dicks. I beam.

I pull back out into the houseroom. My head is covered in clear shells. I realize I am still carrying the sheath of skin I'd pulled out from underneath me, though in the meantime of my moving it has shriveled and become folded, an origami lock. I cannot make it unfold, can't let me back in.

My fingers furl all in a frenzy. I force a mouthful of the skin into me, the eye gazing hard into my back. I choke a bite of my old skin into my cheekspace, chunk it, hoard the whole thing down in one long choke. My nostrils take the evening while my belly rolls the rope of that. Guts in my guts, compiling and scarfed up. I feel it fall back out of me below again. The same skin, lubey and groaning, one shade darker, older blown.

Where I heave to kick the skin the skin sticks to me around my leg, my skin a shoe, then a short legging, a pair of pants and shirt, my skin over my skin again, through in mussy order, out of lack. I can't get the fit to fit me rightly, every centimeter off by half an inch or more. Or less. More shit shitting out of me there underneath me and still sticking up a hominy of whoops.

The eye is laughing. I turn around to see the eye. Its wet sheen bumps over from where I went into it and led. Its reflection appears damaged, yammed up. Pumping pillows.

Inside the eye, another house.

Memory deceives one, slipping creation before creation. Sight pixilated by sentiment, sentiment pent by sight. Neither demurrer nor conviction uncharges one or the other, for in no conjugal truth does truth lie. What pronounced gilt adorns each petitioner, put there by an unparalleled veneer of bright thought. But such verdicts as these verdicts are overlapping slights: sentiment's prejudice and sight's occultation, and thus sight sours sentiment and sentiment blights sight. Still, there's no accounting for the odds and ends of real humanity. The brightest of the unfit. A necessary requisite of due process of law is the opportunity to be heard, in a manner which is meaningful, in front of a forum which has an open mind, and is willing to listen to evidence. Adequate notice and an opportunity to confront adverse witnesses must be afforded. One's father, for they insist he is one's father, though he's got nothing on one but a blurry gesture, a thrust, as they say, toward paternity, one's father was a one-legged man riding a bicycle.

In the instant I see the house inside the eye inside the house inside the final house the house is sitting on my palm. It is smoking and has a cling of mayonnaise around it. I put the house into my mouth. I watch its shape slide down the system of my body through my tubes out my central hole into the chud clung with the shit. The house is larger. It is bigger than the eye.

I climb into the house culled from the eye inside the house inside the final house buttfirst. With my head hung out the house's hole I watch the bigger house around it squeal and fuss a mist up from its ribbing to tell me goodbye with something like an organgrinder's glee.

I wave back, too. My hands are knotted. A little slur ripped in my immense and spiny nails grown clean from the nutrition of my manure and glistening with what I don't remember. In the smudge the eye is many and there are many eyes inside each eye. I blow a kiss about a mile wide. I wriggle back like begging, with my mouth full and all the tight house pushing in warm massage against my gumhandles and ribcage struts. My neck stretched as if to pop it. My teeth hunched narrow, gold blood throbbed fat. Some splurge falls out of me behind me mossy, slurping before me as preamble into the house born from the eye inside the house inside the final house.

There was a cap, or at least a limit. Some sort of topping off, a way, or at least a rhetorical device, that would signal stop. As a general rule, independent of statutory considerations, the writ of *habeas corpus ad testificandum* under American law may be resorted to for the purpose of removing a person confined in a jail or prison to enable him to testify as a witness. One once found oneself in a ditch. A hole. A gaper. A gasper. A grotto. A groove. A cut. Slit. Trench. Slash. Gash. One found oneself there and congratulated oneself on the economy of the other's eternal return. Elegant, in a word. Smooth. In an other. Inside the house inside the house born from the eye inside the house inside the final house there is waiting, for me only, a cold horse.

This house is long. It goes on and on behind me in cornmatter of a silk and softing nuggets framed in greeny leaves.

I scoot back. The hole in the house folds shut behind me, sealed like envelopes of cash. I am seated on the horse, its meat beneath me, kissing to my thighs. I stroke the horse's head with both hands and watch it tremble.

The horse's hair is grown into my hair. Where my legs are mossy with my pubism, the horse has flies glued to it, little wires like from house to house. The neigh clogs in my trellis, though I don't know what part of me that is. I squeeze the horse with my ribbed thighs. My thighs make in the slits on his meat together a ribbon of flooding frogs pour loose. A gray, globular stream of chestnut rubbings. It gunks up in a pile, gives steam, a hiss of smoke in letterhead and who is talking. The horse moans with the going of it, making little bristles on his neck.

I move to situate my legs another way long on the horse's throbbing midsection scrolling backwards in the house inside the eye inside the house inside the final house and where I pull my tendons hard against the horsemeat tendons there rips a second and third sleeve-slit according, one with chicken-colored runny cool whip and the other with a sawdust confetti, a cube of leaking purple milk. The spines along the horse's neck grow in swelling again like some cupcakes, cylindrical, a rein. I hold on thick and feel the thick kiss to the matting of my palm, groove on groove and nasty roil.

I hear a flock of birds. I can't look up.

One finds one's stupidity a real asset in collapsing form and function. Say once more. Relevance and materiality are of consideration in such matters. In this way, much of what one is saying is reasonably architectural. Being about egress and exeunt. This right is not violated by a statute which makes the right to the production of a witness confined in prison upon the discretion of the court. Extant lipped round the edges and in the middle, as a river banks, founding the banks of the river. The court could have avoided the issue by first creating a prejudgment writ of attachment to freeze the asset represented by the land in question *quasi in rem* or *in rem*, meaning *a thing*. Similarly, caprice sets certainty, as demonstrated by the effect of gambling on faith, and faith on the come. A question of adequacy of service by publication and mailing of a summons in a partition suit, conforming with the local law with respect to constructive service of nonresidents, naming the party defendant and addressee, 'Albert Guilfuss, assignee' and 'Albert B. Guilfuss', satisfied the requirement of the due process clause of the United States Constitution Fourteenth Amendment, conferring jurisdiction, notwithstanding the misnomer, to render judgment binding upon 'Albert B. Geilfuss, assignee' with respect to a lien upon, or interest in, the land, he having not appeared. Tiffen makes a meal, as mother would say, if there was such a one. The defendant appealed. Thus one discovers discovery. The most interesting thing about him are his long hands. Really, they're quite spectacular. They say he makes the most of roving disaffection, or rather the quick assumption of smooth, fork-tender existence. His future's faultless as his history. Personal, of course. Of course. All history is.

A little pebble wobbles through my belly to my mouth, comes through my mouth and pools there, greases my teeth and cleans my gums, leaks from my cheeks in silent stairwell from my skull hole to some small air section just above me, solidifies and melts, rains on my pants, leaves my skin cold.

The wind of the house around the horse inside the eye inside the house inside the final house wherever any of me am. Shaking. Shaking. A choral halloween through christmas through the day of knives through mirror gift week to birthday doom.

I ride the horse under the shape of someone cradling his or her stomach.

I ride the horse under a year. The year has teeth culled from the dogs and men and others of me in the hours of the night around a pack of ways I moved my body in the recent and high-pitched lasts of light.

In the light we run head on into a screen. A flattened film of randy plastic. The horse brains in his head. From his head there spills a hundred other little horses, thumb-sized, which scatter in the bunk. Each of them zips with a single thread of hair from off the rubdown center of the mesh between the father horse and I.

The horse's brain is black. Its skin peels up around it. My skin tied tight around my arms, the bracelets of the scent becoming every inch I have yet to grow, and pooled up with the scarfing off a hot food that comes pouring from the horse's neck cylinder and chest. The meat as it is eaten instantly into me fits into my body as if it'd been mine: my new voice box, my new aorta and spine.

I press myself against the clear screen. Through its face panel there is someone else. Someone seated with his or her arms held up in arcs. Another color hair bursts from the face. Surrounding in dark room, a blaze from my side washes the skin of the other to a wax, wherein behind, the house around the body way down in here, pulses: muscle, dryboard, lymph. Curtained in deep mink.

My throat's neck bubbles against the panel, the drunk within me wanting any other out.

Behind the enmasked, slathered head another eye sits overlidded, orbited by gulls with beaks as long as I am—or, closer, not gulls but throngs of gray glue, licking by and by—and not an eye, but drugged, dry mollusk, fitted with wire to inside itself convulse.

It's the death risk. The favorite risk, the one that gets the blood up and the guts down. Remember how nicely he wore those twill pants. Hardly imagine he has genitals at all. Or not the rude ones, anyways. A polite prick, standing when someone of some stature enters the room, otherwise well-behaved. Trimmed, in the nonecumenical sense. Not like these. These genitals, such as they may be, are a maggy, moppy mess. They barely stay inside, except when it's raining. Then they tuck up nice. Trained them to go on the paper, but tend to run out of paper, especially in the hotter weather, when the urge for fire sets in something fierce. But not him. The understanding is that he's the nicest man in the world, loves everyone personally, though not indiscriminately. But prefatorily, which is a distinction best made in the dark. The indoor dark. Where haunts the familiar. Difference between history and philosophy. Have long ago been resigned to a vague cabbage-scented loathing, coupled with a heartless sort of want. Made up the mind once to hate everyone, and that was enough. Found that the one act of pure condemnation had the effect of a sort of moral pass, and relieved me of subsequent inquiry, that leads oftentimes to doubt, or even worse, a change of mind. It seemed that loving everyone required more or less constant affirmation, given the state of, well, down there. A fine state, to be sure, but one with, you must admit, problems.

The seated person on the screen's far side strokes the pastry with a leash tethered and in wanting feeding both ways meat on meat.

Inside my cold skin gloves I press my arms against the surface. Where I touch onto the smear my arms click quickly in magnetics and suck down hard against the plane and release air. The air comes from inside me and has the rot again of sweat and money, a cotton candy bleat. It stings. I go to squeal out through my blowhole and bite straight through my bottom lip. The blood sounds like kazoos.

The screen is sticky up against it. I hear a lifting of a bell. That bell rings a ringing in my temple and beneath me, in the house inside this latest house, as where behind me in the room before the screen here the floor begins to sink into the floor. The horse's sagging skin inflates inside the bottom becoming ceiling unto one pervading sky. The horseskin sky holds constellations of a nattered nature chiggered with a crisp set of whinnied phrases locked into its linings. It knocks the machines out of sync.

And I am at the screen strumming through it turning over upside down, and in the mush I watch the seated body hold its posture leaning forward forehead inches from the light.

Clearer then. Here I see he or she is pressing buttons designed in patterns on a plastic lap. Each button is a smaller city cut from pig meat with the wires of a pubic snare.

My whole body coerces through the screen into blue jelly encrusted on the far side with a beep. The bell rings hard in my cerebrum, knocking divots in the floodyards of me where nothing hard remains.

Act of hate or even views not altogether endearing. Therefore, universal love mandated a singular perspective, a kind of heaven-bent understanding, a form of monomania that, with these sagging dragging genitals, was fully incapable of claiming with any recognized authority. No, I wanted the blessed relief that comes from utter lack of comprehension. Like a snail, wanted to boot my house on my back and be done with it. This dovetails nicely with my stay-at-home nature, noted above. I find, and you'll kindly forgive me if I strayed from him, but just for a moment, because he's really what we want to be discussing, or thinking about in any event, him being a sort of North star, not a fixed point exactly, but the point of common reference, if you know what I mean, or, if you'd rather, the common point of common reference. So with this in mind, I'm proposing a center of absolute incomprehension, unmitigated, in the way of birds on a wire.

Ununderstanding.

Where we, meaning me, though you're most welcome to join me, if you think he won't mind. Or notice. Not noticing seems more likely. Less noise. Just the odd scream now and again, and that's easily accommodated.

I once lived off an alley near a hospital and the screaming becomes just part of the everyday. Did I say a hospital? I meant a public charity, of course. Of course. Perhaps it was just another apartment. Hard to say in such light. I've lived many places, and I find the sounds inside sometimes quite difficult to sever from those outside. Meaning him, of course, as he is the outside, meaning the one who more or less sees me.

And you, of course.

What I'm trying to say, and I wish sometimes he could say it for me, he would, and has, I'm certain, repeatedly, though I've forgotten in what case, though not the subsequent sentence, is that I don't understand. That's it. I embrace my not understanding. To the point of overlaying my ignorance with yours. Yours meaning ours. There's no reason to differentiate, after all, leather-bound as we are by the blessing of eternal hate. I don't mean hell, of course. Just the indoors. Domestic violence, some say, as if there's any other. Oh, I know all about war, countries going at each other like blood brothers. But honestly, and just between us, there's enough mutual disregard and self-concern to supply a marketplace of bombings. Between us meaning between them, of course.

Before I forget, I would like to emphasize how very accommodating he's been too, welcoming us, meaning me, like he apparently did, or means to. I say apparently because I don't want to presume, but did think I detected a flutter in the nethers once when he looked over my head. I was on my knees at the time. He was a perfect gentleman, and if memory serves, he smelt a little of garlic, or, not garlic, but sage, yes, sage, I'm certain of it. It comes from the education, and I'm not meaning to make a joke of it, not at all; it takes a refined man to appreciate the possibilities of dialogue. Of possible dialogue. Of a monologue with an audience. Of a monologue to an audience.

So.

My point is that I believe in you. By which I mean this slithery muck I call me, or something that looks very much like me, and certainly smells like me, awful, admittedly. I could bathe, you know. Deodorize. Perfume. Plunge. Of course, then I'd have to get used to the stench all over again. No. This seems more efficient. To reek, really, without shame. Or with shame, more efficient still. After all, my goal is a certain freedom to think one's own thoughts, as if one had thoughts, or had thoughts of one's own, or even one thought of having a thought, though I like to think so, naturally, to think I might have thoughts of a practical and ever uplifting nature. This is phase one. The muck. A kind of ring around any lesion or body pucker I have carried, bulbs turning on beneath them with old white. A pegboard of another series of gleaming pinpoints, a puzzle picture upright on the ground, pooting through glue. Primordial, that's what he'd say, if he thought to say it. I suspect he's as inspired as I am by the thought of inspiration. Or by the thought of nothing. Barren like my mother.

I once tried to make something, you know. I had a fistful of pork fat and some dry grass, and I wet myself, which was warm, and warmth is conducive to particular generation, and I shat, but just a little, enough to build some sort of small hut, or low platform.

Pins and prisms in my forearms.

Boating in my hands.

My head sucks buttered neatly through the surface between me and this other posture snug of no gesture. The light inside the room inside house inside the eye inside the house inside the final house goes blonde.

My first arm through the screen's face fans up fleshing in the color making more. Inside my arm, the cords of televisions, knobs of hot sauce, liquid shit.

My shoulder sputters with the spit up, sprays rupture on the inseam of the coming room inside the house with blush where in the multi-crotch of where the meat's split there is a rise of second color, bone, and a small wink of a third translucence, tissue punked with musk.

Behind me at the screen the million tiny horses have returned, the color of the tether-hair made bluer and a tremor in their eaves. On each horse a little man rides barking at me from behind. Slightly larger dogs nip at the men's heads and crush the horses underneath their wag-whirred feet in song commanding me to stay.

My chest part through the screen now turns the flesh clean inside out. I am ribbed inside like a condom clung with mother juice and pearls.

The other body now kneeling in the room here in the bathe-glow holds both hands hard to hide its hidden face cordoned with rings. The black blouse around the upper body slick with resin, the muscles taut and spasmed underneath. Monotonic chanting shakes the wall. Lip rasp. Rye bread burning.

The thrumming mollusk begins to open up its wings above the body's head. Barren, like my mother. What now, she said, when she meant to say what next. Squatting pondside, she never bothered to lift her haunches, no matter how deep the rise. She thought she'd had the last laugh, and she had, for what I'm really interested in is the irredeemable, or that's what he tells me anyway, and I suspect that's so, given my respect for him, and for the aperture in my eyes. It's a small thing really, no lids, not a bother even except in heavy rain.

Behind me dogs are eating dogs. Horses malfunctioning in growth speed, some with mutated limbs, some balloon skulls. The house around them and my last backside stutters with a loss note knocking down the walls, wherein behind each I can see by turns the rooms I've come through, this final final room, the screaming eye, the house around the eye, the final house around the house around the eye, and beyond that there, a trust: the knit of chrysalises in mansion around the whole hull of any other inch I've breathed upon. I am stuck. A clasp of nodules where my want wants, framing a stasis. The colors of the rooms thereunder and refracted splay into my designing shelves of self in movie-tone: stairwells up, uncounted towers, pig meat, money, sand, a color helmet…

The ice must sing inside my skull.

I took to wearing blackface for some time, to stay put, you understand, to be finally fully me. That, I think, is the beauty of damnation. He didn't mind. What was nice was that he continued to wear his hair short around his glasses, giving a kindly feel to the nape of his neck. In this way, he proved himself capable of great hate, and this was comforting, given the wait. That was when he gave his great speech. Have you seen the pictures? I don't have any, but from what I hear, everyone had the look of a heartbeat. Before he spoke, I saw him put a piece of gum under the chair, and I don't think I could have loved him any more than at that moment, for the fixed fact that he had chewed and moved on. That was ambition, that was the real deal. Spearmint, I would imagine. Me, I'm a traitor to such resistance. A bitch. I'd like to say nigger bitch, but that would be just bragging. I've no real authority in the art of naming. Not like him. He's the real master of original intentions. Note the small hairs on the back of his hands. See how they lie all in one direction.

The other body raises, inside the light, its melting hands. The prayer spit lathered to them all worked and burning through the flesh. Burned. Bedded. Made into a man. He would have certainly thought on it, as he now thinks on it, it being something, or nothing, implying the something that it isn't. But my point is that I do have legs, which means I don't. So in this way, I am perfect. As perfect a fragment as statuary. And don't you think he has the most beautiful hands? Infinity will be the end of me. Mog is him is him is him is Mog. In every particular a man. There, done and said. No more. Certainly. Certainly Mog, of this certainly. Mog is him is him is him. No farther. Here. One. One is Mog. Call for infinity. No more. Again.

The other body speaks a language and I feel me speak it too.

How his or her voices comes out: as nettle, the feathered feel of ghost moth wings and boiling water, a crag of magma-paper vessel that spread across our distance in a pipe, and once before my face splits into two, a bifurcated stem sent each way to wrap around my pierced lobes and latch on. Once surrounded, cupping full to fill the image of the horns through which my days of sound have died, a pistil seeks down into each, left, right, and plugs itself somewhere deeper in all purring rashed against the smallest bones in my whole body with a xylophone of shudder.

What words burst through this pipe: [the voice is detuned, boxy, several pressures all at once; a pump of syllables as through a tuba that has taught itself to talk like cold celery being bit through, the snap of vessels as invented upon impact with a dove.]

In the left ear: "Drug Me" by Dead Kennedys b/w noise of someone reading off the names of women who were scalped in the outlying regions of downtown; in the song itself, another set of lyrics laid into the honking, extremely slowed down voice, words I cannot make out but in bibble and sores that rise along my tongue.

[Hearing the hearing makes my wounds heal. My blood ceases spilling, among which we have become so encased we are rounded, as at the center of a hill or in the mound of some massive star about to burn out to collapse upon itself, unshow its meat. The blood room thick, unlit besides the glisten in his or her and my unblinking eyes.]

In the right: Dogs barking; baby urine; a cartoon played in reverse; the last words spoken by Lenin on the shitter before he stood to last raise the thick lip of his pants; a screwdriver; a child reciting numbers; the dialogue of my whole life; the dialogue of your whole life; a pig's living body thrown again again against a pile of wood.

[I try to respond here but the seal is so much where my skin is making me boxed in and the slip of walls in room around us growing there where again I can see into the State-wide light, its color crushing up along the stemcage of our fortress at first in tendrils of the veins along a leaf, and gathering in fat around each, milk riding the line there spreading slick into long holes through which I can see the infestation my whole home has become, a pillar of fly salt rising up in column to support some lidless edgeless lordless ceiling underneath the x'd-out sky.]

He creates plausible scenarios and makes them so. Me, my body is a vassal, forgive the consonant. Though I don't mind, of course, and isn't that your cause and effect, neat as a halo. But honestly, the past is simple, reduction in the death works. In this manner, god, if there was one god, and not the twenty-odd, could be considered composed of coupons, percentages taken off the price so long as you can afford the paper. It's a peaceful process of self-fulfillment. Rather, it's a peaceful process of self-debasement. One or the other, or both. In this way, I imagine we, meaning we, resemble the jellyfish. A colony more than a creature, a communion more than a communication. Spineless, of course. What do you think? By which I mean to say when. We should ask him, next time we orbit round. We were talking about my lack of procreation. Acreation. Anti-creation, if I could stretch myself to real curiosity.

The sky by now: below us oozing. His or her words writ already in the newly growing speck of rising fields of what will feed us pumping upward from the broiling soil fed in blood that rains up from us and the other oozing from my double's pipe-fed sobbing mouth.

More blood. My mind. Glue in color olding. The eyes inside me, all at once.

The rising lids. Cold gore: ham in slivers, prostates, another field of nipples, pickle paint.

Passing my groin and buttocks through the screen's face I loosen a wet cloth from my hole. The cloth's crepe clings to my blue lining, pulling out on me within. The shift of pinch and dishes. Mutton. My lipids rising in a tent. Shit in a sweet cylinder.

Some small moment between me and me clasps around the room and blinks a snow from any hour falling in the crispness of a wink in slow motion through the hold on of the nothing leapt in pause. The prayer around me chokes no whisper, becomes pleasant white paint gloving my arms. And then in the brink of stopping seeing for a second I am in the stitch again.

The dogs make cream.

The stretching slick around the dog cream, smoke holes, jumping in numbers one by one by two by three by five, another rashmake for each of my more obvious corrections, which my skin counts by growing tines. My fingers grow the mohawks. Kiss me in between shrieks caught with the mask. I cannot hear that I am shrieking...

Butter floor.

Roach nest, evacuated. Columnar babies.

The other body no longer kneeling, no longer round. The arms around me 2D inside the room of ash behind the screen inside the house inside the eye inside the room inside the final house.

Inside the none. The portrait's portrait.

Gold milk squirting through gray rods. Her arms and my arms rattled. The mollusk having bloomed into a cone, a thousand petals each with fresh veins blooming off the bloom again. And in the bloom again the bloom again and the unfolding of the locks.

Dog moths. The sound in perfect circuses around my last lengths on the far side of the flatness, old toenails curled up to my heel caked with small crowns in influxed lesion building walls on walls, which in coming through the lipface of the screen's partition catch and come and splinter off to light on other holds to feed into the flooded surfaces and take root and build more.

The other body's teeth. The cavern of my blipped skull where ours touch, lighting the room around us fit with hives, and inside the hives a convex mirror set with punctured center through which unblink another several hundred eyes. And in the mushing of my body through the screen's sink to stand face to face and cheek to cheek against the other sternum, the inhale of the eyes' mouths, come to drink.

When I move, the other body moves too, but not in the same way. What corkscrewed loop of buried gestures in our lungs of the same air. A hiss kissed in the prisms of the engorged mollusk at our heads, pinchers aged and popping off into another, cells of bread.

Where in the house inside all of these surrounding houses, there is no sound for any move. My mouth makes crimp and sour in the image of the other body's frothing and no language will spill out. For each word bloated in the house here there is a floor. The construction rises towered downward through the earth and through the pig and horse and through the belly of the revolving and through the stop.

The other body's spine. Where in any instant never touching here or with the cells of cells slithered side by side inside the neon and gone light there worms another darkness in my brother mirrored in wordless spasm unto me. The eyes blowing a light back arrived in sudden bursts in which the room is seen ceilinged an unending evening tall and wide as my fat inside my sickest dream, the mirrors packed into my beef. As his or her body bends beneath the mollusk large as any life in chandelier caught my cords I hear the harp, too, wedging deeper in the folds of folds like cowered plants. The underbelly of an ocean. Or some breath mints. A cage inside a cage.

My me inside a laugh. Snurting my ass off.

The snot pours from holes, no skin under what speaking left deleted for the bite. Scented in the red of the other's rub marks and the incoming humpsound of birthing floors in the sound the snot arriving and written in the snot, another sight compiling, my final message from the bear hid in my hair.

The snot enwraps my head, another helmet, another helmet underhead.

Another head under the helmet. I blow the purple trumpet: *onnnnnnnnnnn*.

BANG

BANG

BANG

OPEN

AHAHHHHAHHAAHAHHAHA HAHAH HA HAHAH HA H HAHHAHAH AHAHHA HA HHA H A AHAHHHHAHHAAHAHHAHA HAHAH HA HAHAH HA H HAHHAHAH AHAHHA HA HHA H AHHA AHHA AHHA AHHA I have to know how to get back here when I am done with wherever else there is. One has to know how to HOW TO HOW TO get back here get back how to get back when one is done with wherever else there is whatever else.

In the helmet laugh the purring tendrils the curling kissing walls on walls. Black and red striped flags. The cube's blood flowing. My cube again then. My cube then. My me and the me in me and me and me in me in me in me.

The other blinks once and is beside me. Takes me by the meat. Takes me by the center of me. Is my center. An eliminating roar. In money printed with the visage of the mollusk on our skin of skins of skins. This cold. The screaming, drying pigs and horses flat and flatter in the grist. The gloves of nod in helmet locked to the guitar: black on black on blacker music'd nothing overhead, strings vibrating in the ceiling and the wallpaper taught to breathe. The lungs of this house with their old alveoli, blackened to the core. To the brim enough that in my overflowing (nostrils: pig white; mouthhole: blue as no night at all; our single exit: rubber color; all my pores: another snow).

The blooding walls.

The bells.

The body in the other body flooding sewn in sullen smoke and ribcage grind and pouring skinsand from the vents and floors rising in the tower of the tower of night.

The screen behind me already darking nowhere underneath the mollusk sun.